SEESAW

TIMOTHY OGENE
SEESAW

Swift

SWIFT PRESS

First published in Great Britain by Swift Press in 2021

1 3 5 7 9 10 8 6 4 2

Copyright © Timothy Ogene 2021

Text design and typesetting by Tetragon, London
Printed in England by CPI Group (UK) Ltd, Croydon, CRO 4YY

A CIP catalogue record for this book is available from the British Library

ISBN: 978-1-800-75016-6
eISBN: 978-1-800-75017-3

For C. Ogene, SES and JPH

1

LOCATED on the twenty-first floor of the New Tower in the historic centre of Port Jumbo, the Coastal Humanities Club has been around since the late 1950s when it started out as the West Africa branch of London's Art and Reform Club. The old building, designed by a prominent English architect, disappeared a decade ago, replaced now by the New Tower, a modern high-rise that houses various thriving ventures: hotels, oil services companies, IT companies and a host of e-commerce firms with names as vague as the services they deliver.

I spent the night in a boutique hotel on the third floor, where I busied myself at the cocktail bar, 'preparing my notes' for the lecture I was scheduled to give the next day.

There was no need to put me up at the hotel. I lived in the same city. Two bus rides away. But the Club was swimming in money, and I'd long since lost the moral urge to refuse the generosity of those who appreciate my work.

The more I drank the more the title of my lecture changed, from 'Thoreau as Post-Colonial Example' to 'Worlding Walden: The Thoreauvian Stance as Discursive Contribution to Anti-Colonial Thought'.

I'd not read Thoreau in years and I knew little about post-colonial theory. But I'd since perfected a 'mode' of speaking that 'positioned' me to effectively 'reproduce' the 'forms of knowledge' that are relevant to the 'discourses' of the 'Global South'. I had a list of catchphrases that I'd harvested from articles in prominent journals and magazines, with the intention of dropping them as 'signposts' to 'foreground' my legitimacy while 'unpacking' the contents of my lecture.

One of the catchphrases, 'post-colonial psycho-manic modernity', came from a talk delivered at the same Humanities Club many years ago, by a Pakistani historian, who, as I saw when I looked him up, was now the head of the prestigious Provoost Institute in New York, founded in the early 1960s by a Belgian-American oil baron and art collector who wanted a space for 'enlightened ideas' that would 'illuminate' a world devastated by the world wars.

The Coastal Humanities Club, which counted the Provoost Institute as one of its 'global partners', was itself a society of civilised men, more or less the African descendant of the European Enlightenment, a belated stop in the World Republic of Letters, situated nonetheless in the centre of a city so chaotic Voltaire would have had a hard time thinking.

As I lugged myself down the hallway on the twenty-first floor on the day of the lecture, hungover, feeling the softness of its thick rug, I felt like I was reliving my childhood in the nineties, walking down the same hallway in the company of my father, dragged to cocktail parties and dinners at the Club, enduring talks on the fate of democracy in Africa, by speakers from far-flung places: Cairo, London, Cape Town, Delhi,

Istanbul. And in the sixties, when my grandfather served as the Club's first black president, the talks and lectures centred around the Cold War, and the Club chanted its non-alignment, ostensibly detached from capitalism and communism, but the cases of wine from 'friends' in Europe were perfectly OK, and members had no qualms importing their bespoke suits from London.

Unknown to them, or so they claimed, the Paris-based group that sponsored their debates and soirées was a front for the CIA, and some of their guests and lecturers were spies from both sides of the Cold War. It was my father who told me this, how his own father had written letters and articles to try to salvage the Club's reputation.

One time, walking down the Club's hallway with my father, he stopped and lifted me up to see a group photograph on the wall. He pointed out a man he described as 'a famous English novelist' who 'came through our city in the seventies', taught creative writing at the university, and gave talks at the Club. The novelist had turned out to be an agent working on a joint US–UK mission. I was twelve or so at the time when he shared this with me. That photograph, with the rest, including portraits of my father and grandfather, is still up there.

'Someday yours will be on that wall,' Belema, my agent slash manager, said to me when he delivered the news that I'd be giving the Club's New Voices Lecture.

He'd done the legwork as usual, and had prepped me in advance, warning me to shelve my grudge against the Club. Whether I liked it or not, he said, I was now – and always had been – a part of 'the establishment'. And he intended to 'milk the hell out of it' for our 'mutual benefit', especially now that I had acquired an 'American dimension'.

The first thing he did when I returned from the US was to offer me a two-book deal to write about my experience. He had sold ten acres of prime family land outside the city to pay me a small advance. He bought ad spaces in national newspapers to announce the deal, and he made donations to institutes and think tanks across the country in preparation for my future book tour. 'I'm thinking ahead,' he said. 'When I knock on their doors next year they'll open.' The plan 'is to make you big here', and then 'sell rights' to major publishers in the US and the UK. 'Big money,' he said, and I admired him for his strategic thinking. I admired him the way I never did before my journey to the US. And it was this admiration that fuelled the speed at which I began work on my two-volume memoir of life as experienced in the United States of America:

Running Loose in a China Shop, or Surviving America One Misadventure at a Time

and

Seductions of the 'New Rome' or the Journeys of a Barbarian in the Imperial Centre.

My lecture at the Club was 'drawn' from the two works in progress, a fact that was as far-fetched as some of the 'encounters' in the memoir.

As I later gathered from my agent, the lecture itself, which I delivered with so much confidence that I almost believed every word, was funded by the Marshal Foundation for the Humanities, an American organisation with headquarters in Washington DC, a revelation that made me chuckle in delight as I squeezed lemons onto my plate of shrimp and eyed the line of expensive wines and champagnes in the corner of the lecture hall.

After finishing the shrimp, and with a glass of wine in hand, I stood by the wide glass wall, looking at the city as it lay below, sloping towards the Atlantic Ocean, curling and relaxing as the mid-evening sun warmed it.

I was in this contemplative mood when a hand rested on my shoulder. 'Beautiful, isn't it?' It was Dr Mohammed M. Bukoram, once described as 'the best post-colonial social theorist of the black Atlantic'. He said something about the city as a 'multi-layered temporal space where times converge, where one form of epistemology is superimposed on the other'.

I had a faint understanding of what he was talking about, or thought I did, how the Middle Ages could still be glimpsed in broad daylight, in the lives of children shitting outside their makeshift shacks, as the twenty-first century cruised by in the latest SUVs, or looked on from the twenty-first floor of the New Tower.

I replied in the language of critical thought that I had picked up in the US. 'I know,' I said, 'it's a classic post-colonial picture of co-existing temporalities… the past understood in discursive proximity to the present… quite impressive, and symbolic of diversity as both socio-economic and spatial.'

I caught a glimpse of suspicion in his eyes. I excused myself and fled.

I signalled to my agent that it was time to go. He moved me around the room saying his big thank yous to the big men and in a few minutes we were out of the door.

In the elevator going down, he pulled out a bottle of champagne from his leather bag and handed it to me. He had done what I'd asked him to do.

I hid the bottle under my suit and undid my silk bow tie as we exited the building.

We walked towards the car park, where his beat-up Peugeot 504, passed down by his grandmother, waited as our escape vehicle.

The twenty-minute drive to my place lasted three hours.

Sitting in traffic, the windows rolled down, we knocked back the champagne and started out on a bottle of vodka he had in his car.

Halfway through the vodka I had the urge to reproduce some of my ideas for future talks to the passengers in a blue-and-white Volkswagen bus pressed very close to our car.

The noise around us, coming from the cars and lorries and hawkers and shops, meant that I'd have to scream to be heard. The image of my drunk self shouting into the open air repulsed me. I tried instead to steady my gaze, and studied the faces on the bus as headlights pierced the growing darkness around us. I could almost feel the heat they were enduring, crammed into that bus without air conditioning, trapped in traffic, sweating together, waiting as they'd been conditioned to do.

On the other side, my agent was making kissy faces to a woman in a white Range Rover. She ignored him, her windows rolled up.

A hawker carrying ripe bananas and apples appeared between our car and the bus, singing the praise of his goods. A mere child, fourteen at most.

He leaned in and asked if I wanted bananas or apples. I could smell the bananas and the apples mixed with the dense odour of fumes and general rubbish from everywhere.

I said to the little boy, 'Apples are not grown in this country, you know.'

I felt an inexplicable urge to say something different to him, to invest in him the way I could, to shift his mind away from our immediate surroundings, to help him imagine another world. I was experiencing a combination of compassion and loathing, a sense of powerlessness so strong it made me nauseous. I waved him off and reached for the vodka.

By the time the traffic eased I'd passed out.

I woke up the next morning in my room, on my beloved narrow bed, squeezed between my agent and a large woman who looked twice my age. We were all naked. Her enormous legs on top of me, my right leg on my agent's. I sighted the trace of coke on a corner of my desk, next to the takeaway bag from the Silk Road, the new Chinese restaurant a few blocks away.

I wrestled myself out of bed, tiptoed to the window and cracked it open to let in fresh air. The sun was blinding. The chorus of small generators came from all directions, as always, so normal it would be odd not to hear them.

I turned around and saw that Belema had flipped to spoon the woman. I vaguely recalled him making a phone call at midnight, saying something about 'a better package this time'.

The image of the three of us crowded into my narrow bed, tumbling like disposable gladiators in an ancient arena, amused me. It also brought back memories of my first threesome in the United States, an experience that was worth more than the seminars and workshops offered as part of my fellowship at William Blake College in Boston.

Thinking back to the US, and looking at my agent spooning the 'better package' on my bed, I thought of the single phone call that had transformed my life, that made it possible for me to contemplate threesomes as a practice, an act of private resistance in a society dominated by heteronorms and outdated sexual protocols.

I re-crossed the room towards the kitchen, to make myself a pot of coffee.

I paused briefly at the wide G-string and pink bra by the door, next to my laptop.

I looked at the stranger's possessions as if they held a special clue to some puzzle.

I picked up my laptop and entered the kitchen.

The coffee made, I sat down at the new plastic table I bought the week I returned from the US, the same week I installed my high-speed wi-fi and bought a small Yamaha generator. It was all thanks to the miracle of the dollar. I had not had many coming back, but the exchange rate meant that I could afford some of the basic necessities of a modern society. I also installed iron bars on the main entrance downstairs, to keep petty thieves and kidnappers away, and I invested in a new French press and a fancy electric pot.

I poured myself a cup of coffee and began to go through my emails. Nothing important.

I went to Twitter. Three DMs, including one from the North

Rainbow Alliance (NRA), a group my agent had partnered me with to run Zoom workshops on anti-racism 'for those who could not be bothered'.

I was still in the US when he sold me to the Montana-based group as an 'understanding expert on all matters black and ethnic'. He had played up my background as a 'son of the black Atlantic, whose maternal ancestors were descendants of slaves who came back to West Africa'. If Americans were going to devour themselves, he said to me afterwards, someone might as well hide under the table for the crumbs.

My first Zoom workshop for the NRA was delivered from a motel in Nebraska. Following my agent's instruction, I had gone to a local store and ordered an American flag and used it as a backdrop. My audience that day was a father and his two sons, third and fourth generation farmers who'd lived in the same town all their lives, full members of the NRA. Their issue: a tweet from the farm's handle that went viral, a nasty remark about migrant labour.

The boys were in their thirties, their faces concealed in the sort of facial hair Marx would have admired.

Following their example, and to make them feel more comfortable, I reached for the large beer can standing behind my laptop. And we had a delightful time noting all the things we had in common: the love and defence of liberty, and how the world's problems would be halved if more people drank. There would be zero terrorists, I said, if Muslims had a beer a day. I cited study after study in 'journals' and referenced historical events that never happened. I sensed they knew I was bullshitting them; maybe they didn't, but no one complained.

The NRA wired payment to my agent's PayPal, and signed up more members for my workshop.

The following week I zoomed with a woman in Florida who was fired from her job for pointing a gun at a black couple who had just moved in to the RV next to hers. She wept throughout the workshop, speaking her 'truth' of the matter, and I 'co-wept' with her, assuring her that the 'universe' would always absolve those whose actions came from 'a place of good intention'.

My agent had looked her up in advance. I knew she'd visited India and had lived for many years in Albuquerque, where she ran a Native gift shop before moving to Florida.

For her I memorised lines from the Bhagavad Gita, and threw in made-up African proverbs to reassure her that 'authentic' Africans like myself would agree that she was innocent. She left me a five-star review and sent me a personal tip 'for just being human'.

The NRA was a generous client, so the DM from them reduced my hangover by a half. Their social media handler and I had become e-friends of sorts, DMing jokes about the prevailing cancel and call-out culture and how it stifled meaningful conversation. I couldn't care less about these subjects and she, in her early twenties, 'born and raised in Montana', did not particularly sound like she understood the history and complexity of the problems. But she advanced with enough confidence to sound convincing. I went along and grew to admire her steadfastness.

'Could you do a short piece on the situation in Nigeria?' she asked. 'See #StopKillingUsLikeRats and let me know.' She included links to videos and Twitter handles and I followed the links.

While I'd been at the Coastal Humanities Club, quoting Thoreau to that learned society, enjoying their shrimp and fleeing with their champagne, my city was ablaze with protesters marching against a special branch of the National Police Force, a branch that was notorious for extra-judicial killings, kidnappings and unexplained arrests.

The pictures I saw online made my stomach turn.

She wanted to know if I could compare what was happening with the Black Lives Matter movement in the US; maybe the police brutality in the US wasn't just a racial thing?

I'd written a piece along those lines a month or so after my return from the US, a short piece that made general statements comparing racial violence in the US with ethnic and political oppression in Africa, urging my readers to 'de-emphasise race and amplify the human condition as expressed the world over'. The idea was hers and the piece was sold to *The New Frontier*, a politically ambiguous online newspaper.

This time around I couldn't bring myself to contrive a response to her DM. I was shaken by the images of young people in my city making world headlines as they stood up for themselves, pushing back against a society that was designed to dehumanise them.

I closed my laptop, left my coffee and returned to my room.

My agent and the woman whose identity I still didn't know were still asleep, their bodies entangled as though they shared a spine.

I lit a cigarette, went back to the window, and listened to my city as it came floating by in its familiar noise. I closed my eyes and for some reason, perhaps the bite of conscience, I began to think of my 'trial' at William Blake College, the day I was officially expelled from the programme for emerging writers.

2

I saw the dean's office again, and pictured the oak tree outside his window. I could hear his voice and how hard he was trying to stay calm as he tiptoed around the subject. 'We expect two things from our fellows,' he had said that day, trying not to raise his voice, 'to produce work in the genre for which they were accepted, and to attend seminars they are leading or participating in. Your colleagues have all produced work and have actively engaged our students, but you, Frank, have hardly been a part of this programme at all.'

I felt again the intensity of his pain, how he paused to collect himself, relaxing the deep line that had appeared on his brow, adding a layer of sadness to a face already battered by the excruciating demands of academia.

When he continued, he expressed his 'surprise' (meaning disappointment), that I 'came all the way here from Nigeria and could not so much as produce a short story in four months'.

At this point I tried to say something but his frustration got the best of him, turning the rather civilised dean into a little savage.

Raising his voice to counter mine, he continued: 'I recall sending you an email to see what we could do. I mean, how we could help you adjust and deal with whatever you were going through. Your response was, and I quote, "I am on to something." That was in April, Frank, three months after you arrived. It's May now and… I don't know, Frank, my hands are tied here.'

He raised both hands in surrender, brought them down and pushed aside a stack of files, making room for his expansive palms to rest on the ancient mahogany desk he must have inherited from Horace Broughton, the first dean of humanities, whose daguerreotype by Albert Southworth was among those displayed in a case in the lobby.

A giant portrait of William Blake himself, not the English poet, was hanging behind the dean, regarding me that day with a touch of disgust and disappointment. And I swear I heard the seventeenth-century merchant, whose other ventures in the area of human cargo are well documented, mumbling under his breath, 'I did not start this college to offer free rides to ne'er-do-wells from Africa.'

The other committee members were silent for the most part. But I knew they'd all reached a decision: to send me packing for 'non-performance' and 'non-participation'.

Dr Kathryn B. Reinhardt, director of ethnic studies, was especially cold for reasons I understood only too well. She wondered if I had any idea how my 'behaviour' impacted what people thought of Africans. I said I wasn't in America to represent anyone but myself. 'Besides,' I added, 'you have Barongo Akello Kabumba. He does a good job of representing his dear Africa.'

Sharon 'Perky' Hollister was present in her capacity as the academic coordinator responsible for the William Blake

Program for Emerging Writers. She managed to speak, offering me a second chance that we both knew was useless.

'Well, Frank,' she said, 'you've got some time to share work, and we could arrange one or two projects with students over the next few week.'

'What if I don't produce any work or know that I may not be able to deliver?'

It was a thoughtless question. Childish, maybe. But I was already considered a disappointment and I wanted to leave with a bang. I had made a point of showing up late for the 'meeting', swaggering in after two pints at The Snug on Coolidge Street.

At one point during the 'trial' I wanted to interrupt the dean and make him see the bright side of things. Well, I thought of saying, you now know things like this are possible, which gives you something to plan ahead with, you know, a contingency plan for unproductive Blake Fellows. Another part of me wanted to make it clear that I intended to write but found myself in a new world where fiction no longer existed, where everything was so drummed up that my senses began to turn against themselves.

I had applied on the strength of the slim novel I wrote and published at twenty-four, *The Day They Came for Dan*, a coming-of-age story set in a fictional version of Port Jumbo, my hometown on the southern coast of Nigeria.

The novel was poorly edited and proofread, lacking in punctuation and peppered with embarrassing typos ('she' repeatedly spelled as 'shay') – none of which was a deliberate experiment in style. It sold only fifty copies and was already out of print, or 'rare', as Belema, who published it, would say.

And it all began when a copy, possibly flung out of a window by a dissatisfied reader, fell into the hands of one Mrs Kirkpatrick, who was visiting her daughter in Port Jumbo.

She'd gone with her daughter to see the weekly street market at Pipeline Bypass, near the intersection which ran east to a cluster of abandoned Slot Oil & Gas equipment stores, and was enthralled by the way books were displayed on mats, how the booksellers called you to come see the titles. I can still hear the ring of her voice when she phoned to share with me her encounter with my book, speaking as though we'd known each other for years.

I was flattered by that call from a white stranger and fan in Nigeria but also irritated by her intrusion. Her opening remark was startling. 'Hello, is this Frank Jasper, the writer?'

I said yes with a start, more in response to her accent than the question. I should have said no, or at least corrected her: 'This is Frank Jasper, the recovering writer. You should have called five years ago, when I thought I was a writer, or was suffering from an illness that made me see myself as a writer.'

It was a midweek afternoon. I was still in bed. Her call was a wake-up alarm I didn't need.

'Your book stood out from everything on display,' she said after her anecdote about street booksellers in Port Jumbo. 'I bought it and was glad I did. By the way, is that a Yinka Shonibare on the cover?'

'Yes,' I answered, calibrating my brain to match the pace and tone of the conversation. I waited to find out where her call was leading.

'I knew it,' she gushed. 'I guessed it from that colourful Dutch wax.'

What you don't know, I wanted to say, is that my publisher pinched that image off the internet, without consulting the artist or his representatives. The whole book was a complete joke. And just as I was about to inch towards thanking her and hanging up, she fired on. 'It's such a good book, Frank – may I call you Frank? Such a good book. I can almost touch your characters, and boy, how did you get away with handling such a delicate subject, I mean, an openly gay character in a novel set in 1990s Nigeria?'

Well, I thought of replying, there were only fifty copies printed and sold, ninety per cent of which went to my publisher's close friends. That took care of the risks involved in 'handling such a delicate subject'.

I held on to my thoughts and thanked her for reading my work, and for her kind remarks.

I wondered how she read the whole thing without cringing at the errors and the poor print quality. These Americans are something, I thought. They fall for anything and anyone, or pretend to. They flatter you until you begin to see sparks of genius where none exist.

Her enthusiasm that day made me want to reread the surviving copy of my novel that was languishing under the bed, a move that I knew would make me revisit my early twenties, the crisis of culture that marked it, the ridiculous outpouring of Byron, Pushkin, Huysmans, Proust... onto the pages of a tiny novel set in modern Nigeria. The big ideas about the world that I shoved down the throats of my few readers.

I believed then, and still do, that rereading *The Day They Came for Dan* would have plunged me into unthinkable despair, the kind I experienced when I read a copy of the first (and last) print run and spotted the typos. For ten days I barely ate anything. On the eleventh day, I exploded into a rage that I thought I was incapable of. I tore up the book and threw the tatters out of the window. Two months later, regaining a measure of confidence in myself and my work, I ventured to mentally revisit the cursed book; I wrote a review and sent it to *The Ganges Review of Books* under a false name.

In the review, I compared my novel to everything Amit Chaudhuri had written, tracing my influences, pointing out the themes, noting my references to obscure writers and artists, concluding with a taut bombast: 'Readers of Proust will find in Jasper's work the same keen eye for the subtle shades of the human condition.'

The Ganges Review of Books, managed by some chap with an astonishingly long name, responded enthusiastically: 'Dear J.C. Barnes... most delighted to run this review...' And they did, and I visited the website every day while lying in bed and peering into my phone and enjoying the way my alter ego had captured the very essence of *The Day They Came for Dan*.

Two weeks or so later, *The Ganges Review of Books* disappeared from the internet. 'Cannot find host' read the page when I tried to load the website. I refreshed it and was redirected to a website selling Viagra.

That was the final blow. It was clear that my book would not go far, that my hope of gaining attention in the West by way of India was a dead end. Then Mrs Kirkpatrick showed up. 'It would be great to meet you, Frank,' she continued. 'My daughter Iris and I would really like to host you sometime. How about this weekend? It would be nice to meet you in person.'

It was happening too fast. I felt my head pounding, my heartbeat racing. I didn't know how or what to answer. I forced myself to say something. 'Give me a second to check my calendar.' There wasn't any calendar to check. What I wanted was a moment to take a deep breath and relax. I had no appointments to cancel. No place to go. I liked not having things scheduled. The thought of agreeing to meet someone at a fixed time was a major source of distress to me. But there was something about her, something in her happy voice, that already made me feel an answer in the negative would ruin her day, perhaps ruin her entire visit to Africa.

I picked up a book and held it close to the phone, 'flipping' through my 'schedule'. Finding no conflicting appointment, I agreed to meet, a decision that was rewarded by a 'thank you' so loud I had to hold the phone away from my ear.

When the call ended, I sat on the edge of my narrow bed for a few minutes, trying to feel something. Belema, my publisher, had sent me a text: 'Hey Frank, long time, no hear. Got a call from one Mrs Kirkpatrick, Betty Kirkpatrick, I think she's American, she liked your work and asked for your info. I gave her your number. Expect a call from her. Hope you're OK?'

I didn't bother replying. My shoulders ached and I felt nauseous. I knew precisely why this was happening; too much activity, too much external interference. I wasn't used to this kind of attention.

I went to the bathroom and sat on the toilet seat and stared blankly at the open door, trying to silence Betty's voice, which kept ringing in my ear.

3

A week later I found myself in a posh part of Port Jumbo, a far cry from the shithole where I lived, where the houses were crammed up against one another, sharing space with open sewers and vast piles of garbage. The streets were tidy in this other side of the city. You could pick up your doughnut if it fell to the ground and be greeted by carefully watered flowers and tender bushes on your way up. The air was fresh, as if filtered by God himself.

I was looking for 10 King Edward Close, named after Karibo 'Edward' Amakiri, a leader of the Kalabari people in the colonial era.

The house wasn't hard to find. A milk-white building rising above an imposing fence with barbed wire spiralling from end to end.

I knocked twice on the gate and someone opened the peephole, stared for what seemed a lifetime, then unlocked the gate for me. His bloodshot eyes, projecting from an impassive face, sized me up and down, and then he screamed as though I was a whole mile away: 'Ahh yuuu the raitah?'

'I am,' I answered as quickly as possible.

He let me in and spat out something he was chewing. It

made a nasty sound as it hit the cobblestone. I flinched. He frowned and pointed me to the door.

A mere two steps away from him a blue door opened ahead of me, revealing an older woman with a kind look on her face, a turquoise bead necklace with a periwinkle-shaped pendant around her neck, and a pair of round glasses behind which a set of eyes glinted their welcome. She'd seen me at the gate and knew I was the writer. The writer. Frank Jasper, the writer! The whole thing was beginning to sound sweet and enticing. It had, at least, landed me in that posh place, and who knew what else would happen?

Inside, the white walls were covered with locally sourced art – hanging sculptures made from scrap metal, paintings of waterside shanties with the ocean in view, a black mask that was as generically African as it was hideous. A black grand piano stood to one side, near a staircase that curled up into a circular gallery. A blown-glass chandelier with rainbow-coloured petals drooped. I could see my shadow on the hardwood floor, as sunlight poured in through one of two broad windows.

Looking out, I saw a garden at the back, flowers in bloom, and four chairs tucked under a picnic table. I saw my book on the couch, a green page marker sticking out, and I felt a knot in my stomach.

'It's so nice to finally meet you,' Betty said, shaking my hand reverentially with a slight bow. 'Please make yourself comfortable.'

I had imagined what she would look like, this generous reader whose unexpected attention was gradually reviving a sense of what I was, or thought I was: a writer. I had imagined her with short hair, greying, and a few matronly lines under the eyes. But in front of me that day, against my presumptions, was a towering figure with flowing brown hair, slender, with visible signs of hundreds of hours spent at the gym or running the streets of wherever she lived in America, so much younger that at first I thought she was the daughter and not the woman who would become my gateway to William Blake.

She started saying something about her daughter's house, introducing herself properly, asking if I needed anything, tea or coffee. I was too distracted to pay attention, and I nervously answered 'both' to her offer of tea or coffee. 'Sorry, tea is fine,' I corrected myself.

As she went to make me tea, I tried to replay her introduction, most of which I hadn't caught. She was born and raised in Charlestown in Massachusetts, to an Irish family whose ancestors fled some nightmarish event in the old country. Her father was a schoolteacher, or was it a college professor? Her mother was a civil servant who worked for some government agency in Boston. And a few things were said about how rough the neighbourhood was when she was growing up there, how my book had a similar ring and atmosphere, with its range of bleak characters whose lives were constantly marked by violence, the clear line of socio-economic divide between households in close proximity. And then she went off to college to study anthropology, did the Peace Corps in Tanzania (or was it Namibia?), and had since felt a strong connection to Africa; her daughter no doubt took after her. She herself wanted to be a writer, and had in fact started a novel many years ago – a young adult novel inspired by her experience teaching kids in Namibia (it might have been Tanzania) but, you know, life happened, and the novel-in-progress was shelved.

When she brought tea, she also brought a thick photo album she'd put together and often carried with her on trips to Nigeria (clearly for the benefit of her local acquaintances).

The album contained photos of Charlestown past and present, and other places in the Boston area. The Bunker Hill Monument was the first to catch my attention, the way it stood against the cloudless sky, intimidating.

She carried on talking as I flipped through the pages, struggling to conceal my growing disinterest. She provided the commentary, complete with back stories for each photograph.

There was a badly shot picture of a church, which she promptly told me was the well-known Old South Church. Next page, a picture of Blake Hall, the main auditorium at William Blake College. It was here that she brought up the fellowship at William Blake.

'Actually,' she said, 'my husband is a professor at William Blake.'

'Oh,' I said, without looking up from the page.

'You know,' she went on, raising her face in a way that suggested that I take a break from the album, 'you know, there's this great opportunity for young writers at William Blake.'

'Oh,' I said again. I looked up and attempted eye contact but found myself gazing at the window to her right.

I could see how close we were on the couch, and I tried to imagine what else was crossing her mind, whether anything was expected of me in exchange for this opportunity. She was, after all, from a country that popularised the saying, 'There's no such thing as a free lunch.'

'It's an extraordinary programme,' she carried on. 'They started it a few years ago, and they've had writers from India, Scotland, Germany, New Zealand. There was a writer from South Africa, I don't remember her name, I think she was South African, I mean, she wasn't *African* African.' She unleashed a confident smile to underscore her own observation.

I reached for my tea.

The cup was lukewarm.

I took a casual sip and returned it to its place.

'Interesting,' I said.

'And the programme is fully funded.'

'Wow.'

'I know.'

'Generous,' I added.

'You know, I bet they'd be interested in your work. I know they'd be happy to have a writer from Africa. You should look it up and tell me what you think. I'm more than happy to put in a word for you.'

I didn't know if she expected me to leap and dance at the opportunity, and I couldn't tell if my not leaping and dancing disappointed her. What I felt was a weight rising and sinking in my stomach. My palms began to sweat, and the photo album on my lap began to feel like a pot of hot coal.

'Just think about it,' she said, and I replied, a little too loudly, 'I'll think about it,' to which she replied, 'Great,' an octave above my response.

I was about to say something else but she was already onto a new subject. 'So, Frank, tell me about yourself. Do you have family here?'

A dreaded question. How and where to begin? Tell her that I worked two days a week at the post office and two nights a week as a bookkeeper for a seedy brothel somewhere in town? My impulse was to awkwardly recite my Wikipedia entry: 'Frank Jasper is a Nigerian poet and novelist, the author of *The Day They Came for Dan* (Cocoyam Editions, 2008). He holds a first degree in English and History from the University of Port Jumbo, and a Master's in Interdisciplinary Studies from the same university.'

That was the identity I allowed myself, the only thing I could bear to share with the world. The bit about my book was a truce between me and Belema. The Wiki page itself was a serious battleground between us. He'd created the page in those early days of the internet in Nigeria, without my consent, of course, and watched it like a hawk. His original entry included something about my family: '… born into a family of intellectuals, Frank was raised to appreciate books at an early age…' I went in and edited out everything about my family. He re-entered it and I deleted it. I called him to express my disapproval and he denied any knowledge of what I was talking about and then, sounding hurt, inquired: 'Just out of curiosity, Frank, why are you so keen on erasing my thoughtful notes on your very significant family history?'

'So you admit to creating the page?' I asked.

'That doesn't answer my question. You should be proud of your heritage. Those men were brilliant. Fuck what people say. Anyway, let me know if you're working on anything new. I'll publish anything you send my way.'

He saw (and still sees) himself as some John Calder discussing future projects with his authors. He, too, was disappointed when, months later, I emailed from Boston to say I wasn't producing any work at William Blake. He had emailed me back with several 'story ideas', including a two-part retelling of Conrad's *Heart of Darkness*, beginning with a Togolese prince who travels to Victorian England with his servants and takes a small boat down the Thames, from London to Oxford, recording what he sees and stopping for a pint or two with the 'natives'; and a second part where the same prince repeats his experiment down the Charles River, from Boston to Cambridge. 'Loads of post-colonial stuff in there,' he added, to provide context, 'brilliant stuff if you pull it off.' He also encouraged me to write a novel based on my family history. I was not interested and avoided the subject whenever it came up, the same way I evaded the subject when Betty brought it up that day. I didn't want to bore her with a history I wasn't interested in, or find myself straining to show enthusiasm should it prove interesting to her American sensibility.

The Jaspers and their complicated lives go back to the late nineteenth century when a young 'native' named Christian Jasper was expelled from the historic Lairdstown Mission for 'misbehaving' with the daughter of Owen Jasper, the Welsh missionary known for pioneering Christianity in the Middle Belt region of Nigeria.

As the story goes, Christian's father, my great-great-grandfather, was among the first Christian converts in his village, and among the few that learned how to read and write. To honour his new faith and the man who showed him the light, he adopted Owen's last name. And when his son Christian was born, the child was baptised by Owen Jasper himself.

Jasper's own daughter was born in Hertfordshire the same year as Christian, my great-grandfather. Jasper's wife Edith had left the mission once she knew she was pregnant, and she never returned.

While working on my novel and researching my great-grandfather's life, whose story I wanted to extract and use as a strand of my protagonist's lineage, I came across an article on the life of Owen Jasper, in which it was speculated that his sexuality may have contributed to his wife's decision not to return to Lairdstown. Edith's letter to her sister showed a worry about Jasper's 'proximity' to a certain 'learned native'.

Owen Jasper travelled once every two years to see his daughter, Harriet. Years later, he went home to see his family and returned with Harriet, now grown-up and eager to help with the good work on the left bank of the Niger. She planned to stay and teach for a year at the local mission school.

At this time, the young Christian Jasper was just finishing his secondary education at the prestigious CMS Grammar School in Lagos. He returned that same year, in 1882, to teach at the mission school. He and Harriet fell in love for obvious reasons: they were both nineteen or so, educated, and strong believers in the mission to educate the local children and expand the reaches of the faith.

But their open-mindedness wasn't shared by all. People were saying things, and soon enough the young lovers were facing exclusion from the community. Owen Jasper's reputation was at stake, and so was his project. The solution was straightforward. Send both lovers away: Harriet back to England and Christian on missionary work through towns and villages downriver. Christian embarked on that mission, ending up in Port Jumbo, where the Niger empties into the Atlantic, where he would later build a career as a renowned schoolteacher and principal.

Before leaving, Christian was forced to sign an agreement never to return to Lairdstown, and never to contact Harriet again. But Harriet had told him that she was pregnant, a fact that compelled him to break his agreement. He wrote to her. No reply. He kept writing. No reply. He moved on but remained single for many years. He married in 1911. His son was born the year after. He named him Laird.

Laird was sent to a boarding school in England, and later went to Cambridge on a colonial scholarship in 1930.

In England, Laird did everything but align himself with the church as his father intended. He gained a first in Classics and spent the years after graduation travelling through Europe, writing and maintaining the diary he had begun at boarding school.

When he returned to Nigeria, just before the outbreak of World War II, he shunned the church and took up a post at a trading company, where he rose quickly. He never married but in 1951 he had a son, Richard, with the only daughter of a local politician.

Their lack of secrecy threatened the reputation of his father and that of the politician, who, at that time, was eyeing a seat on the regional council.

My grandfather was forced to move out of the old city centre. The politician gave him a house and monthly salary to save face. This was back in the fifties, when Port Jumbo was still sparsely populated.

It was to that same house that I returned after the failure of my novel, fresh out of graduate school, without a job, depressed. The street now bore my family name. The surroundings were no longer as serene as they had been, and the quiet, grassy distance between there and the city centre had long become cluttered with derelict houses and grim shacks.

Back then, my grandfather, Laird, had turned his house into a salon of sorts, where his 'free range' friends came to drink, smoke and read their works. 'Free range' because they all had a similar story to his, born to established families, educated, but for one reason or another, often idealistic, they were disconnected from the world around them. They avoided government jobs and politics, and stayed away from religion.

When my grandfather became president of the Coastal Humanities Club, the drinking and abstract political talks found a second and well-funded home.

After my grandfather died in 1983, the house fell to his son, Richard Jasper, my father, who had also studied Classics at Cambridge, graduating in 1975. He was enjoying his own decade of writing and travelling when his father died. He came home that year, and on his first week back he met the 26-year-old Philippa Conton, a painter and daughter of Benjamin Conton, the Sierra Leonean artist known for his portraits of random Sierra Leoneans in the sixties and early seventies. Benjamin was a descendant of Timothy Conton, a freed slave who had settled in Freetown.

Philippa Conton, married back home, was visiting the now defunct Harbour Artist Colony in Port Jumbo when she met my father. I was conceived that year. Philly, as my mother was called, filed for divorce when she got home and returned to Port Jumbo to be with my father. They never married and maintained an open relationship until my father died, after which my mother, for the first time in many years, returned to Sierra Leone.

By the time of his death, my parents had successfully cut ties with their families, choosing instead to create the world they wanted, existing among writers and artists, living off their inheritance, which, by the time I was out of university, was a mere trickle. They had the house, which was gradually falling apart (and they didn't care).

So, to Betty's question, 'Frank, tell me about yourself. Do you have family here?' I could have shared something with her. But there were old question marks that never went away, that I no longer felt the need to pursue.

For years I lived with the feeling that my family was out of sync with the world. We weren't like the families around us. There was a degree of openness, a disregard for what people might say, that marked my family. I knew my mother's lovers. They came and left the house as they pleased. I also knew the women who came to see my father.

I remember getting drunk at nine, among grown-ups who themselves were too drunk to notice the way I wobbled.

I remember the face of a man who pulled me up to him in a hug that lingered too long; he was one of my mother's lovers.

There was the woman who, drunk at noon and alone with me at home, invited me to inspect the space between her legs.

Then there were the bullies at school who never bothered to beat me up but would, instead, ask me to explain who and what my parents were. 'I hear your parents are not married.' 'Your mother is a prostitute.' 'You father is mad.'

I did wish to share something personal with Betty, though, who had taken the pains to read and appreciate my work. Maybe a word or two about my childhood, which, I deduced, she wanted to know about.

There is the scene in my book where the protagonist arrives at school one morning to discover that his pencil sketches of his parents' friends are hanging on the walls of the classroom, displayed there by the class bully, who'd stolen them the day before. Dan, my protagonist, had sketched them the way he'd imagined them: oversized heads, breasts for limbs. The teacher tells him to take down the pictures amid howls of laughter from his classmates. He goes from one drawing to another, ripping them off the wall, unable to hold back the tears, becoming more aware with each step that his is a life alone. No friends to defend him. Parents he couldn't share his problems with – how could he talk to them about his portraits of their lovers?

I thought of bringing up this scene and sharing what inspired it. But I couldn't bring myself to revisit memories I thought were better left repressed. I did not – and still don't – have the tools to handle the memories of my childhood.

Once, two years ago, I visited a psychiatrist who had recently set up shop in Port Jumbo, a Nigerian mental health practitioner with a thriving practice in the US. The Port Jumbo office was some kind of pro bono experiment affiliated with Psychs Without Borders. I told him how I had responded when my book came out littered with errors, and he asked how much of the book was inspired by my life growing up. I lied and said none of it came close to my childhood. The look on his face showed that he caught the truth in my lie. He said something about a second session. I agreed but never went.

If Betty expected to hear tales of growing up in Africa, all the classic examples, she would be disappointed. Mine was in a genre of its own.

I offered her a vague response: 'Well, I had a split life, you see, my parents were free-spirited intellectuals. I grew up with books and smart-sounding people. They left me with a strong interest in culture, and almost nothing else.' I gave a fake laugh, self-conscious. 'In a way,' I continued, setting down the photo album, 'in a way, they courted the margins, and raised me to do the same. I guess that shows in my work, you know, that desire to represent the margins, to reproduce without bias the things that are silenced by the noise of so-called progress.' I waxed a little too confident, if somewhat dry, careful not to be too intimate and personal.

'Interesting,' she said and drew back as though to brew a line of thought but said nothing to follow up, which came as a relief.

Interesting. The way one responds to a remark one couldn't care less about or might care about but would rather not apply the tiniest amount of intellectual rigour to. But Betty struck me as a different creature. To her the word 'interesting' meant precisely what it was supposed to mean. Still, I wondered if she wanted more. All I gave was a fleeting remark, but it struck enough of a chord and led to a second invitation, this time to join her and her daughter's friends for drinks the following weekend. 'Bring copies of your book,' she added and I stiffened. There were no copies to bring. Just *the* copy gathering dust under my bed.

The last time I googled myself, I saw a copy was floating about on abebooks.co.uk, sold by a bookseller in Lowestoft in the UK, and it was going for three hundred British pounds, with the sad inscription: '1 of 50 copies EVER printed, rare, signed by the author, with original errors.'

A year before, my publisher had spotted a plagiarised French and English combo-version on the internet, published in Algeria by a young (and frankly more talented) writer who modestly described himself as 'a neo-existentialist man of letters'. And his was doing better. He had more than a hundred Amazon reviews. I had two: one by my publisher, disguised as 'an Orkney-based follower of new African voices', and the other by myself, disguised as Olu Dayo Genes, 'a contented ex-priest, happy cynic and lover of all things black books'.

The conversation with Betty fluttered and fell on the subject of my character's last name, Seesaw. She was fascinated by this name, and wanted to know its origin, since it did not sound particularly African. I wanted to tell her it was a made-up name but decided otherwise. I didn't want to disappoint her.

'You will find variations of the name,' I said, 'along the south-eastern and south-western coasts of Nigeria. There are Essos, Sisas, Seasons and even Seasalts. Of the different etymological explanations, the most popular is the one about a group of seventeenth-century Spanish adventurers exploring the areas around Pico Basilé, the highest peak on the island of Bioko in what is now Equatorial Guinea. The explorers had taught their local guides to say *Si, señor*. Mispronunciations led the Spaniards to make matters easier for the "natives". *Si se*, it became. Over the years, those "natives" associated with that group of explorers were nicknamed *Si se* or *Si se'or* by the other "natives". By the late eighteenth century, the nickname had become a legitimate name, passed down and written in various forms, making its way along the West African coast.'

She believed every word I said, or else feigned belief so well I saw it in her eyes, or thought I did: that glimmer of expectation. And this unnerved me, especially the vibe I was beginning to get from her, the idea that she wanted me to linger and share more. I sprang to my feet and announced that I had someplace to go.

She followed me to the door and stood there watching me count my steps to the gate. I avoided eye contact with the man at the gate, who was now sitting cross-legged on a rocking chair, tossing peanuts into his mouth, listening to the BBC on his transistor radio.

4

O N the walk home, I kept beating myself up for not sharing more with Betty. I passed a flock of teenagers taking selfies with their cell phones, puckering their lips, all in front of a new fast-food outlet, Mr Cheese Bistro, modelled after McDonald's. So much change, just as I had shared with Betty. The city had transformed itself from a quiet coastal town with layers of colonial history to one bursting with fashion houses, supermarkets and fast-food chains. Old houses were disappearing, replaced by modern apartment blocks.

I passed the main library, which stood at the point that used to mark the old city's main entrance. It was closed that day, and I saw a group of shoeshiners on the steps.

Walking on, I thought of Betty's offer to 'put in a word for' me. There certainly were Nigerian writers scattered across the United States, and many more in Lagos and the bigger cities, with critically acclaimed books. She must have read the big names. Why take an interest in me?

I caught a reflection of myself in a glass wall.

I slowed to look without making a full turn, just a sideways glance.

I saw the shape of my stomach, how it sat below my chest, not exactly sagging but getting there. I felt a compulsion to run all the way home, to shed a few calories. But I thought of what I would miss, the sights and sounds.

Back at my place, I poured myself a drink and wondered what I might eat.

I looked around the kitchen as if I was seeing it for the first time. The last time I cooked, about two weeks before, I was still twenty-nine and the rainy season was just beginning.

The stove, sitting on the kitchen floor, needed kerosene and new wicks.

There was a tuber of yam under the kitchen island, next to a ripening bunch of plantain.

On one side of the kitchen island, a wilted bundle of pumpkin leaves lay next to limp carrots, evidence of my attempts to eat healthily.

There were oranges in a square wicker basket, standing between a bottle of palm oil and an empty ceramic vase.

I sipped my drink and approached the vase, an object that had always been there.

I rubbed its narrow neck, grabbed it and felt its porcelain coldness.

I let it go and paced around the kitchen.

The word 'bachelor' came to me. I dismissed it. The word 'domestic' came to me. I dismissed it.

I gulped down my drink and went out to buy kerosene and wicks from street vendors.

On the way, I saw a new kiosk advertising phone cards, and a sandwich board that screamed, *Make Your International*

Calls Here: USA, Europe and Canada. There were hundreds of such kiosks scattered across the city, and a few on the east end of Jasper Street. Nothing special about this new kiosk. But I found myself paying it close attention. It was the USA that now seemed to pull me in. It prompted me to replay my meeting with Betty. I tried to imagine myself in the United States. A roster of images flooded my mind, all from the books I'd read about that country. I knew my Hawthorne and Stowe, my Melville and Poe. Twain and Henry James I'd devoured. Cather. Baldwin. Faulkner. Bellow. Updike. Cheever. Auster. Morrison. Roth. Hemingway. Dos Passos. Fitzgerald. My mind kept churning out names, and an imaginary America that was both distant and near began to form.

My father and grandfather admired the US but never visited. They both had the strange habit of reading novels and memoirs by Europeans who wrote about America. They saw themselves as an extension of Europe, and somehow felt the best way to admire the United States was from a privileged distance.

Later that evening, after dinner, I pulled out my laptop for the first time that week. I dusted it and placed it on my desk. I looked in the drawer for my USB modem. It was exactly where I had left it, unused for days. I removed the SIM card from my phone, inserted it into the modem and powered up my laptop. I impulsively looked up at the electric bulb, as if to gauge how long before the next power cut. Out of habit, I googled myself and ran my eyes down the first page. Nothing new. I went through the search pages, 2, 3, 4, 5. I typed in 'William Blake Writers Boston'. Contrary to what I had thought, that the programme was new and therefore unknown, I was surprised to see it listed on major artists' and writers' residency websites.

I landed on the home page and checked the application requirements: a personal statement, a work sample not exceeding twenty-five pages, two references and a proposal detailing the scope of work to be done. To be eligible, one had to have published a book – a novel or a collection of linked stories, a novella or a collection of poems. The applicant had to be below the age of thirty-five, and had to reside outside the United States.

Curious, I clicked on *Past Fellows*. I skimmed their statements and proposals and couldn't tell if I was impressed or jarred by their confident declarations: how sure they were of writing, finishing and presenting what they were proposing to write; how they wanted to challenge this and that with their writing, contest 'systems of thought', and 'complicate narratives'. I leaned back and thought: What will I contest or complicate? What do I want to challenge? No answers came to me. And even if I had the answers, how would I phrase them to sound like those I was reading on the website? They all seemed to have a way of speaking, a shared vocabulary that hadn't made its way to my world. A past fellow had proposed to 're-narrate and re-negotiate the relational dynamics of climate cultures through the fictive impulse as discursive and reconstitutive'. Another was putting together a hybrid novel intended to 'simulate (while undermining) the spatial violence of anthro-social histories'.

I clicked on *About Us* and was greeted by a welcome note from the director, Professor Colin Kirkpatrick, with his picture at the bottom right, his face widened by a smile the size of a glacier. Betty hadn't shared much about her husband. I googled him and saw his faculty profile: a graduate of Boston College and Boston University, he taught Intermediate and Advanced Fiction classes, as well as intro classes in Twentieth and Twenty-First Century American Literature; he'd authored a book of essays on the art of the personal essay, *Speaking Up Close* (Maple College Press, 2001), and a novel, *Revere Beach* (Comatose Press, 1984). I looked up *Revere Beach*. It was described as a novel about a middle-aged professor and father of two having a secret affair with a Japanese exchange student.

There was a picture of Dr Kathryn B. Reinhardt, listed as co-director of the programme for emerging writers, though her domain was primarily the programme on ethnic studies. She also taught creative non-fiction and had published a memoir, *Meet Me Halfway* (Arctic Zebra Press, 2014), and a monograph on early indigenous women's writings in the Midwest. I was about to google her when I remembered my data plan might run out.

5

THE next week, I went to Betty's party. The house was already full of guests when I arrived, and I was greeted at the door by Iris, Betty's daughter, who was in reality the host of the party, since everyone present was either her friend or linked to her projects in Nigeria. I was meeting Iris for the first time but soon enough was floating in her company, moving with her from one guest to another. There I was, 'Frank Jasper, the published author', leaning into her, shoulder to shoulder, like childhood friends. She filled the room with her presence, her light-grey dress cut just above the knee, tailored to match her frame. Her guests didn't care who I was but flashed their teeth and shook my hand, their heads cocked or slightly tilted – 'Ah, a writer' – and carried on with their conversations. The simple fact that I was a writer was sufficient reason for me to be there, even if no one actually wanted to talk to me. I looked the part as well, wearing a second-hand shirt missing a button at the top, baring a sparsely hairy chest, which all added to my charm and character as a creative type. The guests were mostly Europeans and Americans stationed in and around Port Jumbo for one reason or another, 'expats' as they called themselves, in their mid- to late thirties, with ivory-white teeth and smooth skin. A dangerously tanned redhead with wine glass in hand was saying something about her ex-boyfriend – 'He was a complete cunt' – but swiftly gave me an innocent look when Iris and I approached. A heavyset woman with green eyes, looking awkward and out of place with a dusty brown fanny pack strapped to her waist, introduced herself as Doris, a South African conservationist working at a local wildlife sanctuary. I wanted to ask a question or two but Doris exuded a confusing mixture of skittishness and coarseness that forced me to move along. When I landed in front of Mr Maduka, the other Port Jumbian present, I suddenly began to feel the weight of my odd presence at the gathering. He was standing alone by the window, overdressed in a three-piece suit that did little to conceal his enormous stomach. He pinned me down with his stern stare, and instead of shaking hands and moving on like the rest, he ran his eyes from my worn-out leather belt to my beaten-out-of-shape shoes (passed down from my grandfather). Then, in earshot of everyone, he boomed, 'So you are a writer, eh? A novelist, eh? What have you written?'

'What have *I* written?' I asked back.

I could hear the hostility in his voice. He didn't wait for an answer from me. He charged on, parting his legs for balance, as though to wrestle me to the floor, and started peppering me with more questions.

For a second I began to imagine what he was up to. It occurred to me that he wasn't asking these questions for his own sake but for the benefit of those around us, perhaps to unmask me as an impostor, and in doing so remind me that my type – visibly lacking the material lustre of the moneyed sort – does not mingle with 'expats'.

Iris had been sucked away by the redhead and her animated account of her ex. And as these things tend to happen, a centripetal force drew to the scene the person I least wanted to see me humiliated: Betty. She was just in time to hear Mr Maduka unleash another question: 'Have you read Pascal Nwabuko?'

I haven't and won't, I almost blurted out. But before I could gather the courage to reply, Betty was already speaking.

'A fantastic writer,' she cried. 'I read his novels before leaving Boston.'

'He's the best African writer of our time,' Mr Maduka added, turning towards Betty and offering a smile, unleashing a layer of charm he hadn't shown me. 'You know,' he boomed, 'Nwabuko might just be the new Chinua Achebe, and I'm sure he'll make the Booker shortlist this year with his new novel.' Then he turned to me, resuming his contemptuous demeanour. 'What do you think, eh?'

Before I could speak he moved on to some other subject, dropping names of other known African writers. I scanned the room for Iris, caught her eye, and excused myself from the company of that confidence-busting idiot, who, I later gathered, was an investment banker with strong ties to a scandalous oil company.

'Have you been up to the balcony?' Iris asked when I reached her.

'No, I haven't,' I replied, relieved to be far from Mr Maduka.

'It's nice up there around this time,' Iris said, inching away from the redhead and her break-up story. 'I'll show you.'

We walked up and with each step the wine-fuelled murmur of voices faded. I began to feel like myself again, free to remain in my head.

'A perfect view,' I said. From where we stood the cacophony of city traffic was a muffled hum, almost like the sea when heard at night from a distance.

'Indeed,' Iris said, closing her eyes and drawing in a lungful of air.

I surveyed the row of rooftops and saw a number of small shacks tucked between and behind fancy houses. Turning to the left, down below, I saw a group of men in the garden of Iris's house, four of them, clutching their beer like lucky charms from distant lovers. It wasn't hard to figure out who they were: drivers who chauffeured the expats around and beyond the city. I could see how they bore their important jobs in starched and neatly ironed shirts and trousers, in polished leather shoes, with clean-shaven faces that nevertheless betrayed years of suffering. They seemed satisfied where they were, outside, while the young expats wined inside. At least they weren't commercial taxi drivers battling thugs, fumes and the stench of drunken passengers.

As I was looking, a young maid brought them a tray of barbecued chicken skewers. The men released a little cheer, leaped off their chairs and pounced on the tray. Relaxing again, they planted their lustful eyes on the poor girl as she retreated, tracking her rear until the door snapped shut. Iris had seen this too.

'My mother can't stop talking about your novel,' Iris said. 'Looks like you've got yourself an American fan.'

Self-conscious, I stared down at my feet. When I glanced up I saw an undecipherable grin on her face. I summoned the courage to speak. 'I guess that's the point of writing, the hope that somewhere, somehow, a reader will enjoy the work.' I was paraphrasing a line I'd read or heard somewhere.

'She thinks you're a talented writer,' Iris said. 'She knows her stuff, having tried her hand at it.'

'I'm flattered,' I said, easing into my best conversation mode, resisting the urge to ponder the last bit about her mother's attempt at writing. A failed writer with an instinct for good writing? I wasn't sure if Iris was being ironic or condescending or both.

'And she does run a book club back home,' Iris added.

'I see. What kind of books do they read?'

'They just pick from the *Times* bestseller list or anything on *Oprah*.' She said this with a little shrug and her lips signalled something I couldn't decipher.

'So you'll apply, right?'

'Apply for what?' I asked.

'The writing programme in Boston?'

'Oh, well,' I said, avoiding her eyes, 'I'm still thinking about it. Sounds like a great opportunity.'

'Let me know if you do apply,' she said. 'I probably won't be back there for a while but you never know, I may be around to welcome you.'

'I'll let you know,' I said, and asked how long she'd lived in Port Jumbo.

'Almost three years now,' she answered, 'on and off. Funny that I've been here for that long and hardly know the city.'

She looked out to the horizon, as if to scan the entire city and shrink it into a small screen.

The sliding door opened and Doris, the South African conservationist, stepped out, looking like she'd just run a marathon. She planted herself between us, her back facing me, and proceeded to give Iris a long hug. An exotic fragrance that I couldn't place filled the air.

'You're missing the action,' Doris said, still with her back to me.

'I'll be down in a bit,' Iris replied.

When Doris returned downstairs, Iris said, 'That's Doris for you, always making sure I'm OK.'

'I suppose that's what friends are for,' I said, shocking myself with my ability to carry on this sort of conversation. I thought of wheeling the conversation back to where we were, to Iris's hint at seeing more of the city, the real Port Jumbo, outside the cocktail bars and fancy restaurants where expats went to mingle. Perhaps I could show her around. But I couldn't picture her in the places where I went: waterside bars with wooden walls and giant speakers blasting out songs at the entrance as the river washed up near the door; or those makeshift restaurants that popped up after dark to support a nightlife that the likes of her would not see until they really went looking. I avoided the subject.

'Why Nigeria,' I asked, 'and not, say, South Africa or Kenya?'

'Good question,' she began, and then paused as if to organise her thoughts. She held the railing with both hands, pushed back and looked at me, all in one quick and elegant movement.

'Why Nigeria,' she repeated and turned around to lean into the railing, folding her arms. 'You know, I've never given it a thought. I worked in Botswana for a year and lived in Zimbabwe for a few months. At this point it doesn't really matter where I am in Africa.'

A thought crossed my mind: she could be a spy. I took a new look at her, trying to spot one thing that would confirm my suspicion. I wanted to ask about her job in development consulting, the nature of which her mother had mentioned the other day: meetings with top government officials, public–private partnership programmes that gave her access to leaders of industry, travel to state capitals around the country and consulting trips across West Africa. I felt a small palpitation as I tried to formulate a question that could lead to an unspoken gotcha moment.

The maid appeared behind us and informed Iris that it was time to head out to the French restaurant a few blocks away. So they had plans for dinner elsewhere? I had no idea. 'I thought it was only drinks and snacks?'

Iris turned smoothly and said, 'Oh, it must have skipped my mother's mind, but you're welcome to join us.'

I declined. How in the world would I be able to afford dinner at a French restaurant in Port Jumbo? And why suffer the humiliation of Mr Maduka's reaction if he saw Iris or her mother paying for my dinner? I had a few deadlines to meet, I lied. An essay to finish for a local magazine, which made sense to her since I was, after all, a writer.

'We could hang out next week or the week after,' she said, 'if you're free.'

I pulled out my phone. 'Let me see what I have this month,' I said, as if I had anything going on. I found no major commitments 'the week after next' in my non-existent calendar. I agreed to meet.

On the way downstairs, walking behind her, I had a quick look at the half-open bedroom to my right and saw a sprawling bed with light-blue sheets, tidy and illuminated by a calming florescent bulb. I spotted Doris's fanny pack at the head of the bed.

Downstairs, I emptied my glass of wine in one savage gulp, said my goodbyes, and left.

I took a bus to Morgan Street – named after John Morgan, the Scottish poet and missionary – and walked towards Morgan School, founded and managed for years by the same poet.

I turned right and walked the length of the eastern promenade, listening to the ocean and hoping to somehow overcome the anxiety that had accumulated during the evening.

At the Brass Street intersection, I saw two men playing cards in front of Bartho's Pepper Soup Joint. I took an empty plastic chair and sat where I could watch the players and also see the ocean across the promenade. They asked if I wanted to join. I declined and bummed a cigarette from the one who had invited me to play. The sound of drums and trumpets and horns could be heard in the distance, coming from the far right side of the promenade. A parade. Soon they'd approach and linger, then head into the city. It could be one of many things: a funeral, a coronation, a political rally. I wasn't in the mood to endure the noise up close.

I stood up and left the card players and ended up at the seedy SoSo Bar at the top of Brass Street. It was still early evening and from here, looking out the window, I could see the sun reaching down to the ocean, growing larger as it made its grand departure.

I ordered a bottle of Heineken and drank slowly, mindlessly watching the silent television as the loud music punched my ears senseless.

I knew that in a few hours the bar and the other bars on Brass Street would transform into outdoor restaurants, with tables out on the street, putting an end to traffic, and certain types of city creatures would emerge: workers from the factories, the unemployed with no hope of employment but a robust appetite for cheap liquor, the young and restless with more energy than society was willing or capable to harness, prostitutes who made no effort to disguise what they were selling. All united by some unrestrained quest for pleasure, rebelling against the new middle classes and their moral pretensions.

It was my first visit to Brass Street in a long time. I'd been a regular when I was at university, and had spent even more time there when I began work on my novel. Recalling those nights, and unsure of what to make of my experience at Iris's place, I decided to wait for darkness to fall, to drown myself in what the night would offer. And when it was time, I found myself outside, sitting at a table on the kerbside, with three heavily rouged women who were already plastered when they joined me. They were loud but so was everyone else around, voices competing with the speakers pumping from all sides. The ladies told jokes about 'last night' and I laughed as if

I cared. The one to my left kept slapping my lap as she spoke and the one to my right would lean into me as she laughed. For a second nothing existed outside that moment. Not my novel. Not the possibility of going to America. Not my job at the post office. I wanted the night to go on until my breath was no more. But somehow, as the night pressed on, and as the ladies talked among themselves and laughed and drank, I heard a voice rising from that beautiful chaos: 'So, Frank, tell me about yourself. Do you have family here?'

I finished my drink and stood up forcefully, staggering back, stirring a minor protest from the ladies. 'Where you dey go, fine boy?' they asked. I said, 'I dey go piss for that corner.'

I caught the sound of my own voice, how it stood apart from theirs. I knew that they, with their trained eyes, saw through me and could tell that my dalliance with the night did not evolve from the same depths as theirs. I saw pity in their eyes. I distanced myself from the table and began to walk away, faster than necessary.

It was nearly 2 a.m. when I got home.

I flung myself onto my bed.

I drifted in and out of sleep and finally found myself wide awake at 5 a.m.

That voice returned to me again: 'You know, I bet they'd be interested in your work. I know they'll be happy to have a writer from Africa. You should look it up and tell me what you think. I'm more than happy to put in a word for you.'

I stood up and went to the empty bookshelf where I kept my cigarettes and lighter. I took a stick and went to the window, pushed it open.

The city was quiet, amplifying my thoughts. I was considering Betty's suggestion. What would I propose to write, and what would I say in my personal statement? How personal should the personal statement be? I'd have to seek reference letters from my publisher and also from my boss at the post office. The former would happily oblige. The latter had no idea I was a writer. There would also be visa issues to sort, which meant that I would have to gather documents to prove my citizenship and also guarantee that I would return after the fellowship.

And as I listened to the silence outside, I saw the bright colours of autumn, the spectacular conflagration of trees singing the end of summer. I'd 'seen' it in books, the magic of watching snow fall from grey skies in winter, the fog in early spring. I might as well apply. No harm in that. A wave of certainty crashed through me. I tossed the cigarette and went back to bed.

6

THE next day I called Betty and said I would apply. She shrieked her excitement and said I should do so as soon as possible. The enthusiasm in her voice killed my resolve. I waited two weeks, prompted again by Iris's text messages, inviting me again to 'hang out'. I was under attack by mother and daughter. I thought of places to take her, places that weren't too raw and removed from the places expats went. I thought of routes to take on our walk, routes that wouldn't lead through my neck of the woods – walking with a white woman was a sure way to lose my anonymity.

We agreed to meet on a Saturday afternoon and spend the rest of the day together. I had an itinerary: start at Okadigbo's by the university, a small palm wine and pepper soup joint run by Pol Okadigbo himself; walk to Ofor's Collection; and explore the old art district while staying away from the shithole neighbourhoods that included mine.

Okadigbo, or Chief Okadigbo as he would insist you call him, had been until recently a professor of history at the University of Port Jumbo, where, for more than two decades, he taught the history of China in Africa from the Middle Ages to the present. Before that, in the seventies and early eighties, he was a research associate at Makerere University in Uganda, where he wrote a bestselling book on the Indian Ocean slave trade.

Setting up Okadigbo's was more of an excuse to bring his retired and retiring friends together for drinks, to recreate the faculty clubs they'd known all their lives. It wasn't unusual to find them hunched over bowls of goat meat pepper soup lamenting the fate of Africa.

It was at Okadigbo's, years ago, that a certain professor of cultural anthropology, mourning the lack of interest in heritage preservation in the country, choked on a morsel of goat meat and died.

Iris arrived on time, wearing a white skirt with tiny sea-blue stripes and a white sleeveless tank top with a round neck. The place fell silent as she walked in and squeezed me a hug. I knew what they were thinking. Where did the white woman appear from?

It took me a minute to recover from her hug.

I caught a waft of that same exotic fragrance that was on Doris, and wondered if Iris had just been to see Doris, or the other way around, or if both women simply happened to use the same brand.

I'd picked a table in a corner, near the window, and asked if she was OK there or would prefer to be outside. Outside, she said, causing me much anxiety. I was aware of the attention her presence would generate. But outside it was.

We found a table and sat down.

I scanned the area and could see the rising interest from all quarters: shopkeepers across the street standing in front of their shops, looking with keen eyes; students coming from (or going to) the nearby campus casting curious looks; men standing around the newspaper kiosk making no attempt to hide their curiosity. She just might be, as I was beginning to realise, the first white woman to plant herself at Okadigbo's, perusing the menu as though she was a regular.

There were areas in town where her presence wouldn't raise attention, and areas where it would cause pandemonium. I had chosen Okadigbo's because of its location – not too posh and not too shithole.

The colour drained and reappeared on her face as she studied the menu. I wondered what it was that affected her this way, and what the changes on her face meant. Was it the goat meat pepper soup? The cow tail pepper soup? The popular 'Jumbo Assortmento', a mix of goat and cow entrails? Was she a vegetarian? A vegan? A pescatarian? I should have asked.

The waiter came, a middle-aged man with a sequence of ethnic marks criss-crossing his cheeks. Smiling, he asked what we wanted to drink – beer or palm wine. We both went for palm wine. Food? She closed the menu and said she'd pass. I wasn't interested in food, either. The prices on the menu were on the high side. I was grateful to whatever made her pass.

Our palm wine came in a vintage demijohn, frothing to the top. I poured her a glass, and watched as she studied the milky white drink. By now we'd already gone through our initial catching up, which basically centred around my impression of the other day at her place. I'd mumbled something about liking the atmosphere, about it feeling warm and friendly, and she'd brushed it aside and said she no longer wished to throw such parties because it reinforced the expat culture of networking among themselves instead of exploring and connecting with their 'host communities'.

She took her first sip of palm wine and paused to assess the new taste.

'Where does it come from?' she asked.

'It's tapped from raffia palms,' I said.

She sipped again, and cocked her head as if to pair the taste with something else she'd had. I waited for her verdict. She changed the subject.

'How often do you come here?'

'Once or so a week when I was a student.'

'Oh, the campus is just round the corner, right?'

'Yes,' I said, pointing at the sign to the university. 'I did my undergraduate and graduate degrees here,' I added.

She asked if I was the only one in my family to study here. It was a complex question, packed with tributaries, and I dreaded it. She could have asked: 'Do you have siblings? Are you the first to attend university in your family?' The question could have taken many forms, but she'd condensed it into a single line that left me with the responsibility of untangling its many strands. I gulped a mouthful of palm wine, contemplating an evasive answer. 'Well,' I finally said, 'I'm an only child.'

I asked if she had siblings.

Yes, she said, a brother named Shannon, who was adopted after she was born.

Was Shannon back in the US or someplace in the world as she was in Africa?

Well, the last time she heard from him, he was 'bouldering' in Cuba.

'Interesting,' I said.

Indeed, she said, and gave details. Shannon had a difficult time as a kid growing up. He was always in trouble. But in college he fell in love with a 'super outdoorsy' student from Wyoming, and they began travelling the world together doing what they loved, from climbing mountains in distant places to jumping out of planes.

She shifted the conversation back to me. 'So, what do you do when you are not writing?'

I surprised myself by talking about my job at the post office, about my life before I wrote my novel and how, after graduating, I worked for a few months at the university bookshop just around the corner.

Randomly, she asked how much alcohol there was in palm wine, holding up the label-free demijohn. I couldn't say. No one talked about percentages when drinking palm wine. She could feel something kicking in and thought it was maybe best to stop.

I cleared my glass and suggested a walk to Ofor's Collection.

We turned right onto College Street, now packed with students hurrying back and forth in the late afternoon heat.

Feeling spontaneous, I decided to take a different route from the one I'd intended.

I led her towards Nembe Quarters at the east end of Port Jumbo.

The closer we got to the Quarters, the denser the air became, as if someone was pumping dust. The houses, too, changed in appearance and style as we progressed, from the well-maintained detached and semi-detached houses around the university to derelict tenement houses with peeling paint and clothes hanging on windows and balconies. Shacks also began to appear, their wood and zinc walls visibly weak and ready to fall if faced with heavy wind or rain. We were three turns away from the main street. Our shoulders touched from time to time. Her phone rang. It was her driver calling to see if it was time to come get her.

We entered a skinnier street crammed with dry goods kiosks and makeshift restaurants, or *bukas*, with benches set before low, wooden tables. I could tell one smell from the other as they floated about, the aroma of *egusi* soup wafting in from the little *bukas* on the side streets, and the competing smell of open sewers. Children everywhere, darting here and there. Young men standing at all corners, looking. I was noticing these scenes anew. Her presence had heightened my senses and I became in that moment a foreigner in my own city. I could sense her growing anxiety as we descended into a world she'd only known from a distance: it was one thing to be chauffeured through in a car, and another to be in the midst of it all, vulnerable.

'Oyinbo,' someone called from a narrow alley. 'Whitey,' another voice rang out from a corner. Soon there was a throng of children singing and clapping behind us, tugging her skirt, their mothers laughing shyly on both sides of the tiny street. I felt a moment of panic, worried that a strong-headed kid might pounce and strip her naked.

She managed to stay calm as her fans flocked behind her. I began to wonder what she saw when she looked at these people and this place. How did she imagine them? Did they, in her mind, have an inner life, complex and flawed? Or were they as simple as they looked? And what did they see when they looked at her?

A group of girls came walking in the opposite direction. I could see them sizing her up – her hair, her clothes, her legs. They passed and broke into laughter. I could see people taking pictures with their phones and I knew those photos would soon make their way to Instagram and Facebook, where they would assume a life of their own, out of context. There were angry faces too, cold and hostile, following us as we walked through the grime.

The narrow street sloped sharply, and we could now see the roofs of houses in the distance, gathered clumsily and jagged, without a decipherable pattern. This, I said to Iris, is my favourite spot in Port Jumbo. She pulled out her phone and took pictures. We stood on the side of the street and looked. The ocean was visible from here, a blue expanse just after the riot of corrugated roofs. A long-drawn horn sounded.

'We are standing in the old commercial district,' I said. 'It doesn't look anything like it did half a century ago. Back then, it was busy with stores selling wholesale goods to retailers from across the country and beyond. The old port is down there,' I said, pointing to where the ship was coming in. I wanted to say more, to point out the old buildings that used to house major international stores and the offices of banks and solicitors, which were now crumbling and inhabited by squatters.

This is also the spot, I thought to myself, where the protagonist of my novel, walking home from school, was attacked by street kids, spat at and peed on.

'As a boy,' I said to Iris, 'I liked riding my bike down this slope.'

'It looks dangerous,' she said.

'It does,' I said, and withheld the complete truth: I knew back then that it was dangerous, but I kept going down the slope, fast, hoping to crash, hoping to free myself from feeling different from the other children.

We walked on down the slope, turned left, and in no time the atmosphere was different, quieter. We passed the entrance to the Port Jumbo cemetery.

'Only a handful can afford to bury their dead there,' I said, also noting the colonial history of the cemetery, how it was originally reserved for colonial officers and their local allies. I was careful not to mention that my great-grandfather, my grandfather and my father were buried there.

Ofor's Collection was a few blocks away.

It was closed when we got there. There was no reason for this closure. No one was there to ask. The building itself, standing in the distance, separated from the entrance by a well-maintained lawn, shone in its Edwardian limestone whiteness.

As I told Iris, the collection was fairly recent, started in 2005 by Chief Ferdinand Ofor, an oil magnate who was facing money laundering charges and somehow brokered a deal with the government to make his private collection public. It was the first of its kind in Nigeria, and it consisted of minor works by major artists and major works by minor artists from around the world. An eclectic but little-known collection. Ofor had spent years, going back to the early seventies, collecting art. He'd also commissioned artists near and far, often inviting them over for weeks at a time. It was rumoured that Johannes Günter himself, the German multimedia artist, had been a guest at Ofor's house. I shared this with Iris as we walked away, towards the intersection where her driver, one of the men I had seen at her place, was waiting in a shiny black Toyota Hilux.

When we approached, the driver came down and dramatically opened the back door for Iris, who, a little embarrassed, ignored a gesture that he seemed used to performing.

He stood by the door, ignoring my presence, waiting like a royal guard, perhaps disapproving or jealous of what he must have read as my undue proximity to his American boss.

As Iris and I hugged, her back facing him, I stuck out my tongue and contorted my face to annoy him. His payback came a minute or so later, when he'd gone up and reversed and headed back in the direction I was walking. It wasn't much but the splash was enough to soak the left leg of my trousers from the knee down. I hoped Iris had seen him accelerate as he approached the puddle. I wondered if she'd read the energy between her driver and me, and I tried to imagine what she thought of it.

7

THAT afternoon with Iris renewed my interest in the programme at William Blake. I composed an email with the subject line, 'Initial Inquiry: Emerging African Writer Interested in the Programme for Emerging Writers at William Blake College'. I carefully reproduced the tone and cadence of the previous fellows, noting the 'issues' my proposed novel would 'combat'. I saved the draft email, then took a break to calm my nerves and growing anxiety. The distance between myself and the wording of my email was too vast and alienating. I stretched out in bed, tried to masturbate but couldn't get myself going. I reached for the bottle of cheap whisky lying at the foot of the bed. I took a swig, waited, took several more. Stood up and paced around my room, trying to *be* the words in my email, to embody and reflect the confidence I'd expressed in that initial inquiry.

When I finally returned to my laptop, I didn't care to reread the draft email. I was feeling more confident than ever. I sent the email, returned to the bottle of whisky, and began to dance. The music was in my head. Something very American. I knew what it was but couldn't place the words or the musician. It had come to me the way memories from long ago sometimes appear from nowhere. It was strong and loud, something in the mould of Jerry Lee Lewis's 'Wild One', good rockabilly stuff. I knew I'd heard it in a movie but couldn't remember which. I danced away in circles, drinking to what lay ahead of me, to the possibilities of a new life as a writer in America.

That night I dreamed I was in a small town in the American Midwest, watching bulls running through the town's main street, surrounded by Americans who, in my dream, were all speaking Spanish.

I saw a broad-shouldered man who looked like Hemingway, and it was indeed Hemingway, his shirt unbuttoned, showing a hairy chest.

I felt words bubbling up from my insides, exploding forth beyond my control. He understood at once that I was screaming my admiration for his work and adventures.

I approached him and he approached me.

We were suddenly in the middle of the street, the bulls charging in all directions around us, surprisingly missing the chance to ram their horns up our arses.

He asked what I was doing 'here in America'. He spoke as though he knew who I was.

I said I'd come to write the great African novel.

He held my shoulder, looked into my eyes, and said, 'Son, to accomplish anything, you need balls, not one, not two... tons of balls.'

He lowered his hands to crotch-level and made a squeezy gesture as if to hold and crush those imaginary balls.

I stood where I was, transfixed, the bulls still charging.

I was about to say something when I saw John Steinbeck. He was suddenly there, standing beside Hemingway. Apparently he and Papa Hemingway were travelling the country in Steinbeck's camper, his famous Rocinante.

And the next thing I knew, I was on the road with them, drinking and trading stories as we drove west in search of more adventures.

I slept in the next morning, waking up around noon to check my email. There was already a reply from Sharon Hollister, who I quickly christened 'Perky'.

She'd replied minutes after my inquiry. There were exclamation marks everywhere, punctuating her delight that I was interested in the programme. I could almost hear her standing next to me, burbling with excitement, and thrilled to provide support 'going forward' in my 'application process'.

Out of curiosity I googled 'sharon hollister + william blake' and saw different pictures of the same woman, thickset, always looking straight into the camera, holding the same smile that appeared like an afterthought. I followed a link to her Facebook profile and the only visible picture was that of her aboard a fishing boat displaying a large fish I couldn't identify. I began to worry my email the previous night had been a little over the top, that I could have been less formal and perhaps have thrown in a couple of exclamation marks.

I reread my email and to my horror the last line had two typos: instead of 'the global dimensions of violent histories' it was 'the global dementias of violent hosieries'.

I felt nauseous. I imagined Sharon 'Perky' Hollister and everyone else exchanging emails and discussing my idiocy.

I felt like an unfinished product that had fallen into their hands, a child that needed cuddling and support as he emerged from his childishness. Was that what the whole fellowship was about, supporting the unfinished products of the world? I spent the rest of the day curled up in bed, unable to untangle my spinning thoughts.

What I know now, months after returning from the US, is that the US itself is a work in progress – an idea that would be hard to sell to those who haven't lived in or visited that country, whose image of America is formed from the outside.

In one of five talks I gave recently on American politics at the Institute of Comparative Corruption located at the Eastern Nigerian University of Tropical Affairs, I drew attention to the fact that America 'is great because it understands itself as systematically designed to be incomplete within the current structures of revolving global capital and renewed trans-temporal neo-imperialist agendas'. I'd made up that line while peering seriously at my notes.

The Hemingway in my dream was right: to make progress as a writer, a thinker, a public intellectual, you need balls, hard and resistant balls.

I lacked those Hemingway-ian balls that day as I lay in bed mourning 'the global dementias of violent hosieries'. But I went ahead and applied, a week after the deadline.

When the offer came I thought of reminding them of their own words: 'No applications submitted after the deadline will be accepted.' I reached out to Belema, my publisher. He declared it 'the hand of God' and said something about American generosity and their ability to spot a talent from 'thousands of kilometres away'. By the end of the phone call he'd made me see reason and convinced me to accept the offer.

That night, we both went down to Brass Street to celebrate my renewed status as a writer. He was clearly more excited than I was, announcing that the night was on him, 'drinks and everything in-between, like the old days'.

He was referring to the time he signed me to his small press, without an advance but with so much passion and encouragement I believed he'd make me a star, 'the Nigerian Salinger' as he said in reference to my reluctance to engage with the literary circles in town, just wanting to write my coming-of-age novel and be done with it. I saw again the same zeal in him, flashing in his eyes, as we hopped from one bar to the other, him singing the praise of what was to come. I also saw something else, a layer of pride. I was, after all, *his* author, and my accomplishment was a sign of his ability to spot and cultivate 'talent'. It didn't matter that the book had done badly, that he'd written all the quotes on the back cover. What mattered, as we cleared pint after pint, staggering down the street and into more pubs, what mattered was that the book had survived long enough to decide my next step.

We ended up at SoSo Bar, which at that time of night had become an outdoor bar/restaurant, bustling like the other spots down Brass Street. It was here that Belema, overwhelmed and drunk, cleared a table and stood on top of it, ringing a bottle of beer until there was a semblance of silence, the loud music reduced to accommodate his voice as he pointed and declared me a 'genius', carrying on incoherently before transitioning into a poem about America – I think it was Claude

McKay's 'America'. He repeated something about his vision of me descending into that 'cultured hell' and ascending a 'triumphant writer'. I recall how, in that moment, I saw him again as the poet he had been when we first met. He'd described himself then as a 'private poet with a public mission', and I would later find out that he actively wrote and published queer-themed poems and essays in foreign magazines under a pseudonym. I once followed him home to the crumbling house he shared with his ageing mother, a massive building that was as ambitious when it was built as it was impractical, a brutalist wet dream from an era when the military regime handed out contracts to cronies from all corners of the globe. I saw on his wall, opposite his bed, an enlarged picture of Paul Robeson standing on stage, mid-stride, mouth open, exuding the energy of a seasoned actor doing his job. The Robeson picture came back to me as I watched him standing on that table at SoSo Bar, howling like the ex-Beat poet that he was, and I wondered what chain of events had conspired to transform the political poet into the scheming publisher.

The day I got my US visa, I sat out on the balcony and indulged a series of fantasies about my forthcoming trip. What if I went by sea, I wondered. I used the word 'sea', not 'ocean', since the former sounded more poetic. I imagined myself aboard some *J.M. Austen* or *P.B. Coaster*, embarking at the Old Port in Port Jumbo, surrounded by expats going home, West African students returning to colleges in America, investors setting sail after closing deals. I imagined myself out on the deck one evening, looking out to sea, listening to the same waves the world had known for centuries, the same currents that shaped global commerce. I pictured a corpulent and loquacious American emerging to interrupt my contemplation, to discuss his business of selling underwear to West Africans. I imagined offering him a calm and civilised smile before removing myself to the ship's bar where I would sit and trade stories with a British colonial family going to America for the first time, unsure what to expect but thrilled at the prospect of watching a baseball game. I saw us sailing westward on the North Atlantic towards Puerto Rico, maybe stopping to sightsee in the Dominican Republic before heading further north towards the port of New York, welcomed by Lady Liberty herself.

A month later, on the actual day of my travel, I shared a filthy taxi to Jumbo International Airport with a woman hugging a basket of fish-smelling clothes and two men yammering about local politics.

The forty-five-minute flight from Port Jumbo to Lagos was uneventful. I slept all the way. On the flight from Lagos to Amsterdam, a grandmother 'on her way to welcome another grandchild' kept leaning into my shoulder, sleeping and releasing gas intermittently.

The flight from Amsterdam to Boston was different. Woah! Air, a new airline trying too hard to make a name for itself. Their hostesses would have put runway models to shame.

Preparing for take-off, I kept wondering if the rapt attention given on this occasion to safety instructions was typical of international flights. It certainly wasn't the case on the Port Jumbo to Lagos flight, where travellers ignored everything and chatted away as instructions were shared. But on that Woah! Air flight, I saw men straining to see how to properly inflate their life jackets should the plane go down.

About an hour to landing, the woman on the aisle seat, to my right, began to talk. 'I always forget I can unbuckle this thing after take-off,' she started, dragging me into a conversation I wasn't keen on having. Was I living in Amsterdam, she wondered. Oh, just connecting? She'd always wanted to visit Africa. She'd done Morocco, and quite liked it there, but it wasn't sufficiently African. You know, as in real Africa.

When I managed to ask where she was flying from, she beamed and said she was returning home to Syracuse, after nine months living and 'performing' her work in Europe.

She paused, sighed, and said something about returning to a world of 'excess', a line that disconcerted me.

At this point she was looking right into my face, holding a broad unnerving grin, her large eyes unblinking. I didn't know what to think or make of the disconnect between her serious statement and the casualness with which she spoke.

She returned to her snack, something hideously green that looked like plantain chips.

She crushed each chip at the same rate, with so much vigour her jaw muscles tensed and quivered. I followed this motion, timing her bag-to-mouth and crush routine. When she broke this ritual, she inhaled deeply as if to relax her nerves.

It appeared she truly meant what she had said about her country, that it caused her much pain. This realisation, which came to me in small doses while surreptitiously observing her consume her snack, threw me off balance. I'd originally read her words as one of those indirect statements people make to seem modest, like dismissing a well-off background as a way to draw attention to the same. I also felt she needed something more from me, perhaps to reassure her that I wasn't one of those who judged Americans by the actions of their government or their large corporations or whatever.

She asked, 'Is this your first time coming to the US?'

Yes, I answered. She went on to apologise in advance for her country, and descended into something about 'the long history' of her country's 'global imperialistic practices'.

At this point I felt it might have been better to leap off the plane than endure the remaining time to Boston.

As if reading my despair, she moved the conversation to 'her creative-critical practice as a performance artist' who 'uses the body to highlight stories that are neglected by the mainstream'. Her 'practice', she said, was lodged 'at the intersection of critical body-positive studies and conceptions of Otherness'. She made air quotes to show that 'Otherness' wasn't, in fact, *otherness*. She'd just finished a show in which she managed to trap a cold can of PopDiet between her breasts for an hour, lying on the floor of a gallery in Reykjavik, to 'highlight' the company's hideous practices in Guatemala. And to 'highlight' the little-known but tragic 'cultural consequences' of yoga tourism in some obscure Himalayan village, she reclined naked on a fainting couch at a gallery in Amsterdam, inviting visitors to pinch her left toe. I drifted into pretend sleep after her 'candle performance' at a square in Bratislava.

■

At the airport in Boston, I followed the line for non-US citizens and non-resident aliens, a long, slow-moving line, where everyone seemed gloomy, as if unsure what awaited them at the threshold. Those in the other line, with their US passports and resident cards, were more relaxed, and had merely to walk up to a machine and check themselves back into their country. I caught a few eyes from the non-aliens looking at us aliens as though we were an invading force of medieval hordes and Germanic tribes appearing from nowhere, pushing into their lands, wielding axes and spears, eyes flashing red and lips dripping the blood of sacrificial beasts, charging forth to plunder, maim and rape.

At the counter, I handed over my passport and watched as the customs officer, tight-faced, scrutinised my visa.

When asked what the purpose of my travel was, I mentioned the residency at William Blake, to which the officer responded, 'So you're a writer?' I sensed a tone that was a mix of mockery and surprise. He scribbled on my passport, stamped it and discharged me.

Emerging from the baggage claims and wading through a waiting crowd, I stepped outside the airport and stood there in the mild spring breeze.

I inhaled deeply and tried as hard as I could to make sense of what I was feeling. The scene of my arrival was so ordinary it felt unreal. This was the United States of America, the centre of the modern world, and I was breathing its air for the first time, unsure what to expect, trying to pair what I'd read and heard with what lay before me: a world of concrete, taxis coming and going, an Asian family hauling their luggage across the road, the man beside me yelling instructions on his phone in a version of the English language I could barely understand.

I'd not booked a taxi in advance, and at this point I wasn't in any hurry to take one.

It was a Sunday afternoon.

The local buses were coming and going, taking commuters to other New England towns and cities: Portland, Lowell, Concord, Cape Cod, Providence.

I watched the buses closely, as if the town names were symbols of a past I had come to find. In some way, they carried aspects of my past, my formation in a family that watched these locations from afar, that discussed them as though each town was a piece of rare china on display. I had with me, buried in my luggage, my father's thick diary covering the later years before his death, and I knew of several entries that mentioned New England towns, mostly in connection to his interest in poets and writers from this region.

I finally shook myself out of my dreamy state, crossed to the other side of the road, and got in the first taxi that approached.

I was disappointed that the driver wasn't Haitian or some ex-professional from a more unfortunate African country. Just a middle-aged white man.

I gave the address, rolled down the window, and like a dog sniffing the air I poked out my head, closed my eyes and inhaled the world outside, which smelled of salt, like the air in some parts of Port Jumbo.

When I opened my eyes, I saw how greyish blue the clouds were, and how everything in sight fell within blue and grey.

The taxi took a bend on a bridge, turning right.

I shut my eyes again, overcome by a sense of smallness as the buildings rose in their cold confidence. I shrank before them, before the broad road itself, before everything around me, the vast newness that was beginning to impose itself on my senses. I felt the conflicting contraction and expansion of my mind, the force and impact of the new. I was *in* the new, consciously aware of it, but the new was already throwing me out of control.

8

THE taxi deposited me in front of Comstock Place, where the Blake Fellows were housed.

Named after a nineteenth-century 'racist nutjob', as someone called him, Comstock Place was designed by an architect who studied with Frank Lloyd Wright at the School of Architecture at Taliesin. Set back from the other structures on campus, and surrounded by a well-kept lawn with trees here and there, the building was designed to look like a stapler, the lower floor separated from the upper by a retreating stretch of space, glass-walled on all sides. In keeping with the principles of organic architecture, the building was constructed to look like it was rising from the ground, its upper and lower levels mimicking the open mouth of a creature emerging from a hole after years in hibernation. The open space between both floors was occasionally used for student events.

The day I arrived, there was a student in a blazing red WB College sweater standing in that open space, looking straight at the walkway as if she was expecting someone. Seeing her there, I thought the stapler was in fact a dragon, its red tongue about to project fire.

■

My Comstockian room was on the upper level, on the left side of a hallway with six single-room apartments, three on each side. It took me several minutes to make the move from door to room. I was intimidated by what I saw, what my American benefactors had placed at my disposal: a bed so large it could hold ten sumo wrestlers; a desk so finely designed I swore to avoid it lest I tainted its purity; a clean wooden floor that I thought was better admired than walked on.

Looking at the slice of luxury before me, I felt a symbolic response was expected of me. Perhaps prostrate myself for a second or two? Or kneel and knee-walk from door to desk?

I pulled myself together and ventured in.

The smell of cleaning detergent was in the air, a lemony scent that was more soothing than any harsh floor and toilet bowl cleaners I had known.

I sat at my new desk for a few minutes, looking out the window, where the stature of John Comstock was visible to the far right of the main entrance. I'd seen him earlier, when the taxi dropped me off, and I'd stood for a quick minute or two taking in the statue of the man after whom my place of abode was named. The sculptor had reproduced what must have been Comstock's robust cheeks, his jaws propped by full sideburns. Sighting him again from a new height, he seemed diminished and alone, his bulky frame leaning a little backwards as if a small wind would tip him over.

On the far left of Comstock was the building I would later learn was the Humanities building, a muscular three-storey townhouse in the Second Empire style, its brick walls bright against the world of trees and lawns surrounding it.

The Humanities Hall, or St Pierre's House, was left to the college in the will of its original owner, the French-American chocolate tycoon, J.K. de St Pierre, whose late nineteenth-century purchase of a small chocolate company in Dorchester made him one of the wealthiest men on the eastern seaboard. I knew the building was there. It was listed on the college Wiki page. I also knew that the Harry Putnam Library, famous for owning the unpublished manuscript of Dreiser's *Brother Kerry*, was situated behind the humanities building.

As I was looking, drawn into my near mythical surroundings, I saw an empty bench between Comstock and the humanities building, and I felt an overwhelming urge to go outside and sit there.

I imagined more days ahead on that bench, me sitting at noon or early dusk, watching students going about their business, taking in the filtered air of my green surroundings, eavesdropping on two lovers standing nearby or listening to the sound of laughter arising from a group of students picnicking somewhere on campus; I imagined myself taking notes there, filling pages and pages with work and ideas for future work.

I kept my eyes on the bench, which now seemed to radiate an invitation.

I resolved to go out later and perhaps, after making my debut bench-sitting in America, stroll around St Pierre, towards Putnam, and on to the William Blake Art Museum, situated to the left of the Library. I thought this would be my first ramble in the New World, an experience I'd long imagined.

Just then, as if on cue, a bulky man appeared, riding on a motorised lawnmower.

He approached and circled Comstock as if performing some ancient ritual, and then wheeled away, ploughing on towards St Pierre, where he dismounted his mechanised donkey and hand-pulled a weed lodged too close to the edge of the building.

Following this act, which he executed with the practised care of a seasoned gardener, he sat on a ledge to retie his bootstraps.

This pastoral gesture, in this bucolic landscape tucked away in a bustling modern city, contrasted so much with the world I knew. I felt a slight headache picturing both worlds side by side.

I left the window and sat on the bed.

I kicked off my shoes and in no time the whole room reeked of my sweaty feet, a familiar smell that reminded me of who and what I was.

The holes in my socks were still there.

The smell of camphor on my old corduroy blazer, originally owned by my grandfather, was still strong, as if I'd just retrieved it from the box where it had lain buried for years.

I undressed and walked into the bathroom, to register the ritual of a first shower in the United States.

I looked at myself in the wide mirror.

I studied the ring of hair around my dark nipples.

I looked into my own eyes and searched them as though they had a message for me.

Just as I turned and stepped into the shower, I heard the blast of a horn, or something that sounded like one. It was so loud it penetrated the walls of the building, rumbling into the bathroom as if to rouse me for battle.

In my memoir-in-progress, I describe that sound as something out of a war from antiquity, 'the rattling cry of ten Celtic carnyces approaching a Roman garrison'.

What it was, when I ran back to the window to see, was in fact a trombone, wielded by a young man who looked like he could be a younger J.J. Johnson, standing alone in front of Comstock, blowing away as though he was paying tribute to the man in stone. But it wasn't the type of sound you made to honour someone, it was more of a call to arms, a series of sustained and piercing notes. For a second I thought it was the prelude to an open air performance, some American reproduction of a battle against the 'Indians' or the British.

Then they began to appear from all directions, chanting, 'Comstock must come down,' carrying placards, pressing towards the site where the call was still ringing out, only this time the player was mimicking the approaching chant. Soon they were standing in various positions around the statue, all in red, mostly young women, clearly students of William Blake.

I saw in that crowd all shades of hair colour – brown, black, blonde, pink, blue – and faces and complexions whose origins I could not place. I was witnessing, for the first time, a range of diversity that I'd never known, that staggered the imagination. It was one thing to know of this diversity and another thing to see it in person. I struggled to make sense of this motley collection of people united by their mission to take down the nineteenth-century 'sexist and racist'. It was simultaneously beautiful and dizzying.

A small group was busy doing something to the statue. Soon it was clear: they had fashioned a noose out of bras and panties and hosiery and tied it around his neck.

I shuddered at this sight, and felt as if the noose was on my own neck.

I staggered back into my room, my heart beating.

I could still hear them outside. And I knew in my heart that there was something to celebrate in what they were doing – a sign of change, a transition from a world where one could launder one's image after years of private or public atrocities, a tradition with a much longer history than Comstock, that was still ongoing, of which the protest was a healthy warning.

I was thinking of slave owners in the Caribbean and the Americas, violent imperialists in Africa and Asia, who plundered and maimed in their domains but used their wealth to court the polite society of Europe, investing in culture, immortalising themselves.

I knew this history, but I was physically and psychically feeling something different, a mixture of dread and embarrassment, as if I had stumbled on a scene that was not meant for me, that I was not prepared to see or conditioned to comprehend.

Later that evening, around 7 p.m., when the protesters had dispersed, leaving in their wake a statue of Comstock propped up on all sides by placards, piles of underwear, the noose around his neck, I heard excited voices coming down the hallway. I knew they were the other William Blake fellows who shared the same floor with me.

They paused midway, just outside my room, and carried on their conversation, clearly about Comstock and his legacy.

The thought of stepping outside to introduce myself was cancelled by the fear that I wouldn't have anything to contribute. And judging from how they flowed together, it appeared they had figured out a way to bond. They had arrived before me, two days earlier, and I imagined they had established their lines of connection.

A voice that I would later recognise as Sara Chakraborty's said something about Comstock's 'violent policies' that had done 'systemic harm to the female body for more than a century'. She spoke in rapid and fully formed academic sentences that blended what she knew about Comstock with 'a broader awareness of the resurgence of hetero-epistemic violence in our entwined worlds of culture and academia', footnoting her observations with a few remarks about 'this exciting new wave of radical leftist resistance' against 'the spectre of right-wing fascistic implosions'.

I tried to follow her words but didn't know how to plug into 'the notion of protest as ontological'. I also got the impression that I ought to be aligned somewhere left of the 'prevailing mood of the politico-sphere', and needed to be more 'radical' and 'engaged'.

I searched through my lifetime of books and every shred of experience that had defined me and I couldn't bring myself to feel anything that was authentically Left or radical, Right or unradical. Perhaps there was a fountain out there where I could be baptised and emerge more Left of Right or Right of Left, 'conscious' of my 'subject position'.

My idea of an American radical protest was ossified and romantic, involving pictures of people in long hair smoking marijuana, playing drums and banjos, and baring their breasts, reciting poems, dropping acid and reeking of concocted lotions and whatnots. But the protesters I saw might as well have been business executives, clear-eyed with state-of-the-art digital equipment.

As I processed the whole scene, I felt like a man trapped between two extremes: the moral obligation to jump in and support the anti-Comstockians, and the equally moral obligation to stand back and try to understand the bigger picture.

What bigger picture? I wasn't sure. I lacked clarity. I was paranoid. I felt alienated by their language of engagement, by the things they knew that I did not, the world and 'worlds' they 'explored', and by the 'intellectual itineraries that made the present moment possible'. I felt diminished, listening to Sara and the rest.

The surrealist short story I had planned to draft that night, a piece inspired by the empty bench outside, in which I imagined myself as an invisible black breast that ventriloquises the sexual fantasies of a nineteenth-century ex-slave roaming the streets of Boston, about the same time as Comstock's reprehensible policies, was now shattered and replaced by a new consciousness of the world of twenty-first-century American protest.

I still mourn the death of that unwritten piece, which I carefully titled 'The Boob, or the Silent Consciousness of a Black Victorian Tit'.

■

That night, still jet-lagged and exhausted from what I had witnessed, I ventured outside. The campus was as bright as day, flooded with blinding lights.

I sat on that same bench.

Someone – one of the protesters perhaps – had left a reusable Starbucks cup. It was the first real Starbucks cup I had encountered at close range, in person.

I picked it up. There was still coffee inside. I smelled it and inhaled deeply.

I tasted it. Its coffeeness was there, but there was something else.

I took another sip, and filed this experience somewhere in my memory. My first cup of coffee in the New World.

9

My first encounter with Barongo Akello Kabumba, the *other* African on the programme, was a disaster. It was at the welcome party, attended by the programme team and affiliated professors from departments across the college. Barongo Akello Kabumba had introduced himself with all three names, as if to stress his authenticity, and he had shot me a curious look when I introduced myself, repeating my name back to me to press his point. 'No native name?' he asked, adding to the irritation that had been building up in me since I saw his profile on the programme website, where his massive smile and Maasai toga contrasted with my black and white portrait in the same corduroy blazer I always wore on special occasions.

It never occurred to me, not even once, that Kabumba and I could be friends. There was something about him that ticked me off.

He had the same Maasai toga at the welcome party, and this time he had a stick – a damned cattle-herding stick. How he got through customs with that weapon remained a wonder.

Grinning from cheek to cheek, offering slight bows to everyone, he was the centre of attention at the party. There were always at least three people chatting away with him, listening as he gesticulated with one hand, holding out his stick with the other as though to hurry along a cow, his bouncy, full-bellied laughter ricocheting off the walls.

From a corner, standing with Deepak Bhakta, the Blake Fellow from Nepal who wouldn't stop talking about his trekking business and his work-in-progress on racist Western trekkers, I kept tossing Kabumba contemptuous stares. I didn't know why. Possibly because he made me look like an undesirable African, a fake. I was baffled by how much control he had over everyone. He could have cut his Maasai toga to pieces and auctioned each for a thousand dollars and they would have fallen over themselves to buy them without question.

When Deepak excused himself to use the bathroom, Kabumba broke free from his groupies and approached me, crossing the room in quick *African* strides. 'My African brother,' he greeted me, clasping my shoulders a little too tightly.

'Hi,' I greeted him back. 'Nice toga.'

'Thank you. My Kenyan friend gave it to me in Nairobi. The Maasai call them *shukas*,' he corrected me.

'Of course,' I responded, shrinking, self-consciously plunging both hands into my tired, un-African chino pants.

'Funny when Africans call them togas,' he continued, standing next to me, a little too close, keeping an eye on his admirers around the room.

Professor Kirkpatrick was standing a few yards to our left, his back to us, chatting away with Claudia González, the playwright from Mexico, whose reworking of Brecht's *In the Jungle of Cities* was already making the rounds of small theatres in New York.

Sara Chakraborty, in full Indian regalia, was holding a wine glass in one hand and gesticulating with the other, and I picked out fragments of something about 'growing up in Surrey as the grandchild of Afro-Asian immigrants'.

'I'm not saying you're not African,' said Kabumba the Ugandan, 'just funny how we post-colonials are wired to see things through a Western lens.'

The word 'post-colonial' rang a sinister note coming from him, especially since I was already having an eerie feeling that the five of us – Sara, Deepak, Claudia, Kabumba and myself – were selected because we were 'post-colonial' writers whose 'worlds' were interesting enough to jazz up the 'conversation' – another word that I was beginning to dread for what it conjured: a room full of intellectuals deconstructing and reconstructing one thing or the other.

'Funny how that happens,' I said to Kabumba.

'So, how did you hear about this programme?' he asked. 'You Nigerians are everywhere. Always a Nigerian at this or that conference.'

I ignored his joke and tightened my jaw for a second before answering, 'A friend told me about it. And you, how did you hear about it?'

'Oh, I got an email from NAPA.'

'Napa?' I asked, irritated.

'You've never heard of NAPA?'

Now he was getting on my nerves. I ignored his question.

'NAPA. Network of African Poets and Authors?'

'Right. Of course. Nice.'

'You should join NAPA,' he admonished me, 'great place to network and connect with opportunities.' He carried on about the NAPA newsletter he edited for three years until he 'won' the Blake Fellowship.

I ignored his remark and tried to change the subject.

'For a second I thought you were talking about Napa, you know, in California?'

He made a sound, drew closer, and in a conspiratorial voice said, 'Funny, we are the only BAMs here.'

'BAM?' I asked, trying hard to conceal my ignorance.

'BAM,' he said again, pronouncing it the way I heard it.

I racked my brain to get his drift. He rescued me.

'They call it POC here, you know, People of Colour. But elsewhere, especially in the UK, it's B-A-M-E. Black, Asian and Minority Ethnic.' He spelt it out for me, B-A-M-E, stressing each letter as if to drive home a point I was not getting.

'So that includes Sara, Deepak and Claudia?'

He ignored my question.

Fragments of Sara Chakraborty's words floated about: '… this oppressive consciousness of the white middle classes, like their upper caste Indian counterparts… that is central to the present onslaught of right-wing pushbacks.'

I scanned the room for anything to latch onto. I saw Perky, who I'd not met formally at this point. She was standing by herself, close to the door, playing with her name tag, which announced her as the Programmes Manager. She looked skinnier than her online photos suggested. I felt drawn to her, to the silence that surrounded her in that space where words were dropping like hailstones, like Sara Chakraborty's 'what we are witnessing on both sides of the Atlantic is symptomatic of a system that is consciously designed to subjugate and colonise'.

Kabumba carried on about his BAM. And when he paused to drink from his glass, which seemed a little un-African in comparison to his attire and accessories, especially the stick, I summoned the courage to launch a subtle attack. 'BAME in the UK, eh? Interesting, have you travelled there?'

Kabumba didn't get my tone. He surveyed the room and began saying something about the William Blake programme, how happy he was to be back in Boston – he'd visited a few years ago to attend a conference organised by the World Youth Alliance for Cultural Freedom and Socio-Political Inclusion. He told me how much he was looking forward to finishing his first novel, a cross-genre work on the lives of sex workers in some coastal town on Lake Victoria. He wondered if I'd read his collection of stories that was published a few years ago as a 'downloadable pdf' by 'a micro-press in Zanzibar', the 'book' that landed him the Blake Fellowship. It was his fourth writing fellowship, he declared, and I wanted to counter with a question: 'Do you need that number of fellowships and residencies to finish a single novel?' He had also attended workshops in Kampala, Mombasa and Pretoria. There had been one in Prague, too, led by some English novelist whose name didn't ring a bell, where he 'workshopped' the first four chapters of his novel. Interestingly, his first fellowship had been in Nigeria, in a small village outside Ibadan, where he fell in love with jollof rice and concluded that Nigerian jollof must be better than Ghanaian jollof. 'What do you think of the whole Ghana versus Nigeria jollof matter?' he asked. I said I couldn't care less about what cosmopolitan Africans cooked up to debate among themselves on Twitter. The word 'cosmopolitan' set him off on another tangent; he wondered what my thoughts were on Afropolitanism. I said I had none.

At this point I knew my hunch was right: the guy had too much energy.

Deepak was back and had cornered a freckled adjunct. I wished he would come and rescue me from Kabumba, who, as if reading my mind, asked, 'What do you think about that Asian guy from Nepal?'

'Asian guy?' I asked, stressing the Asian. 'I've just met him,' I added and went no further.

To my relief, Deepak and the freckled adjunct came over and joined us. And in that instant, as if the universe had decided to favour me, Professor Kirkpatrick, in high spirits, came towards us and, a little too loudly, addressed Kabumba: 'Hey K'boombah, may I steal you for a minute?' He tapped the beaming Maasai impersonator on the shoulder, and they both walked towards a grey-haired woman in glasses standing alone beside the spread of cheese and grapes and cured meat, balancing some olives on a paper plate. She was, as Deepak's new companion shared, a professor of anthropology with a focus on the mating behaviours of 'indigenous' societies in Africa, and she had recently received the Krank Prize for her work on the San people near the Okavango River.

Sara Chakraborty's voice floated in again, something that included her 'Oxford experience' and 'the lingering legacies of empire' and 'the Anglo-American flirtation with imperial amnesia' that her last collection of essays 'confronted'. From a corner of my eye I saw the shape and majestic sweep of her royal rust saree with its gold embroidery. Her listener, who I later learned was a French-Canadian ethnomusicologist and associate professor with experience of working in the Congo, seemed engrossed in whatever she was saying, his eyes glued to her face.

'So, what are you working on?' asked the freckled adjunct, who introduced herself as Chloe. She who would later become a recurring subject each time I met Deepak for coffee at Café Lucy – 'Chloe and I went to see her family in Vermont', 'Chloe and I are planning an interdisciplinary project together' – and soon enough Deepak would inch towards his ultimate intention, to propose to the freckled adjunct who he saw – and he didn't hide this fact from me – as his ticket to becoming an 'immigrant writer' in America. An honest plan, in my opinion.

I responded to Chloe by repeating the question, 'What am *I* working on?' – a tactic I usually employed to buy time while formulating a believable answer.

Deepak jumped in and began to share his big plans to work on a documentary, and I was glad he did. I kept casting glances in Perky's direction. I saw how uneasy she was. At one point our eyes met. She smiled and looked away.

As Deepak carried on, I found myself studying Chloe's face, catching the spread and pattern of freckles on her right cheek. The freckles were reminding me of someone else, a certain white stripper who was flown in from somewhere to open a high-end club in Port Jumbo.

It was Martin, my boss at the Port Jumbo Post Office, married with four kids, who took me to see this stripper. He'd asked the day before, standing behind me at the till, if I'd been to a strip club before. I answered, 'No, I haven't.' He said, 'We must change that, Frank, and we must do so in a big way. You know, a new club is opening up in town, a fancy one, not those smelly ones with smelly bitches from the villages. This one will showcase classy chicks, university babes, and guess what? At the opening on Saturday, an American girl will be up there.' The excitement in his voice was palpable. A customer came in to send a parcel to Finland (or was it Iceland?) and Martin returned to his office, only to emerge when the customer was gone and say, 'Frank, there's a picture of the white girl on their website, see, see.' He handed me his smartphone and there she was, red hair, those Chloe-like freckles on both cheeks, topless, in a black thong, on the floor of a stage, her slim legs stretched apart. 'She will be here in the flesh,' Martin announced.

When I turned to hand him his phone, I saw that my boss, a father of four and a deacon at the Redeeming Light Global Church of Jesus Christ our Benefactor, the church to which he'd invited me with equal enthusiasm, had a slight bulge on the left side of his fly.

What had he been doing back in his office? Exciting himself over the freckled stripper? Thank God we were alone there. 'You should come, Frank. You know what, I'll call the owner and save us two tickets.'

I listlessly accepted his invitation, but afterwards I wondered why he took an interest in me, why he made no effort to conceal his vices and split life from me, why he believed I would keep his secrets. And so we went to the Prime Gentlemen's Club, which oddly sat on the same block as a private elementary school for rich kids, and, true to what Martin said, the stripper was white, but since she didn't address the audience, there was no way to verify her nationality. She could as easily have been Canadian, German, white South African or white Kenyan.

The place was packed, but Martin had managed to secure a table up front, just close enough to see the stripper's young face, to see the constellation of freckles appearing each time the club lights swept across her body.

I would occasionally look around, away from her, and take stock of the entire space, men with thirsty eyes, thrilled by the performance of the Chloe-like stripper, presumed American without evidence.

Just before midnight I said I was leaving, that I had to see a friend in the morning, which was a lie; I was simply tired by the cheer and rowdiness of middle-class Nigerian men.

To Chloe's question, which she'd got around to asking again – 'So, what are you working on?' – I wanted to lie and say I was working on a novel about an English stripper who had a short career in Nigeria, in the coastal town of Port Jumbo. And to make it sound more interesting, I thought of adding a historical twist, to situate it in the past, that it was in fact a real account that took place in the early sixties, just after Nigeria gained its independence from Great Britain, and that the stripper turned out to be a spy in the service of Her Majesty's Government, working to strip secrets from wealthy, cosmopolitan Nigerians with links to the new political class.

But instead, and because the information was already public on the programme website, I shared my proposed project. 'I'm working on a historical novel set in the US and Sierra Leone in the mid- to late 1800s.' I avoided the meta-commentary on how it would 'engage but also undo the global dimensions of violent histories'.

The idea intrigued her. She said, 'Really? That sounds very exciting. What is it about?'

'Oh, it's about George Thompson, the missionary and abolitionist who sailed to Kaw Mendi, in what is now Sierra Leone, in 1848.'

'How fascinating,' she said, her large eyes widening as she inched closer, causing Deepak a pinch of distress.

I feigned the kind of modesty expected of a serious writer, and said, 'Well, it's still an idea in progress,' and was about to add another thought when Claudia González joined us, with a bespectacled and chubby-cheeked lecturer, about our age but balding, in a grey crewneck sweater choking his skinny black tie, a Philip Larkin lookalike.

Carrying on a conversation he was having with Claudia, the Larkin lookalike said, 'Always a diverse group,' nodding in agreement with his own observation, perhaps expecting some multicultural input from the rest of us, the thought of which exhausted me.

I excused myself and walked towards Kabumba and the woman who studied the sexual appetites of primitive Africans, passed them, picked up a paper plate, considered the grapes and olives, lost interest altogether, and walked outside for fresh air.

In the growing darkness outside, I took deep breaths and wondered if it was best to head back to Comstock Place. A group of students – so young – passed by. 'I'll send you the list,' said a voice behind me, 'or you can just look it up online, Top Fifty Books by Women of Colour.' It was the Larkin lookalike coming out the door with Claudia González. I hurried away from them.

Approaching the Humanities Hall, or St Pierre's House, on my way to Comstock Place, I replayed my little conversation with Chloe. I was glad the conversation had ended the way it did, but also wished I had carried on and mentioned the context from which the Thompson story arose, to gauge her response and also weigh my own reaction to that response. I could have said, 'I grew up overhearing my Sierra Leonean mother talking about one of her ancestors who was taught by George Thompson himself,' and then watched how Chloe would have reacted.

According to my mother, that ancestor was a boy when Thompson landed in West Africa in 1848. The boy and his parents had arrived eight years before Thompson, twenty years after the first ship carrying freed slaves left New York for Sierra Leone.

The first time I googled Thompson, I saw that he had written extensively about his experience. One title stood out: *Thompson in Africa, or an Account of the Missionary Labors, Sufferings, Travels, Observations, &c. of George Thompson, in West Africa, at the Mendi Mission* (1852). There was another book, an earlier one, covering part of his life before the journey to West Africa, about his five-year imprisonment in Missouri for attempting to rescue slaves: *Prison Life and Reflections; or a Narrative of the Arrest, Trial, Conviction, Imprisonment, Treatment, Observations, Reflections, and Deliverance of Work, Burr, and Thompson, Who Suffered an Unjust and Cruel Imprisonment in Missouri Penitentiary, for Attempting to Aid Some Slaves to Liberty* (1851).

I downloaded both books and read them without much interest until I found myself thinking of what to include in my William Blake application. I could propose a project based on Thompson's life, I thought. I had a feeling the committee would jump on the idea, considering how transatlantic it was and how personal.

Looking up Thompson's life for the second time, I came across a paper by one J. Yannielli, a historian at Yale, 'George Thompson among the Africans: Empathy, Authority, and Insanity in the Age of Abolition', and I was struck by a small fact I'd missed earlier. Thompson, according to Yannielli, was 'shocked to find a large group of schoolchildren participating in homosexual activities'. A group of gay boys in nineteenth-century West Africa. I pictured the American missionary, who had given up everything to bring salvation to that darkest part of the world, boiling over after this discovery.

But it was not the gay boys who tipped his sanity, nor was it the harsh weather or the evil mosquitoes that cracked his mind. It was the 'crime' of fornication by a pregnant woman that did the trick, causing Thompson to deal the savage fornicator fifty lashes, to the consternation of everyone, including fellow missionaries and proponents of corporal punishment. 'I feel conscious of a growing roughness,' Thompson wrote in his journal, 'of manner and spirit, arising out of my circumstances.'

A Growing Roughness. The title I gave the novel I proposed to write at William Blake, for which the selection committee enthusiastically awarded me a generous fellowship.

Passing St Pierre's House, Comstock Place in view, I tried to reimagine the shape of this non-existent novel, something different from how I'd proposed to write it. The idea of starting at the harbour in New York was appealing. I pictured my three-year-old ancestor and his parents waiting to board the ship, waiting with hundreds of other African Americans, freed slaves at the threshold of a world they knew and the one across the sea from which they'd been alienated for centuries; standing there at the lips of the vast ocean that bore their ancestors and that would now bear them back. I tried to imagine what crossed their minds, what shades of hope, what depths of fear. The world behind them was violent and cruel, but also familiar; the world ahead, although perceived as 'home', was unfamiliar and inconceivable. They were people of the faith, who'd found refuge in the Gospels, and in their hearts it was this faith that would guide them across the sea, lead them through the perils of settling down in West Africa, through new encounters with 'animists and cannibals', as one returnee wrote in a letter back to America. *A Growing Roughness.* The idea was now so strong I felt I needed to put down a line or two before entering Comstock Place.

I sat on the same bench I saw on my first day, and was about to start typing on my phone when I felt a presence behind me. I turned and saw Perky grinning as though her arrival was expected. She had undone her jet black hair, which now rested on her shoulder.

For no particular reason I looked around to make sure there wasn't anyone from the party nearby. The campus street lamps were on, but it was dark enough in various corners that someone could be hiding and watching.

I wasn't sure why her presence raised my paranoia. Student–faculty 'relations', as I read on a campus blog, were a 'no-no'. Perky and I weren't in either category but still I feared I might be breaking some code by just being out alone with her while an event was going on. My worries diminished when she said something about 'the phoneys back there' and how she 'couldn't stand' such events, which was ironic because she had organised it.

I was relieved to know that I wasn't the only one who couldn't stand them. I wasn't sure who the phoneys were for her – maybe the dean and faculty, all of whom seemed to gorge on every word and action of the 'post-colonial' fellows, worshipping them like gods from another world. It was nonetheless refreshing to know she was not on their side like Sara's listener, who I saw flushing with excitement, maybe desire, when Sara said something about 'the politics and long histories of spice'. You would think he was ready to saddle up a horse and race east on the Silk Road to fetch her rare spices from the Orient.

I'd also seen how Perky was standing by herself near the door as if to flee without warning, her hand clasped in front of her – a gesture that had drawn my eyes to her green skirt, which ended just at the kneecap, followed by pale legs that planted themselves in black Oxfords.

Sitting next to me on the bench, my first close company

since my arrival, her legs spoke to me. The green skirt, now drawn up, introduced more skin, which in the different lighting of the street lamps looked enriched. She didn't bother asking why I left but declared how she knew I too was 'uncomfortable back there', how she 'could feel the different energy coming from me', how she saw how much I wanted to 'liberate myself' from 'the suffocation back there'.

I was careful not to make categorical statements in reply.

I tried to formulate a response to the effect that I truly loathed Barongo Akello Kabumba and Sara Chakraborty, that I was dreading the weeks ahead, how their march of authenticity and resistance would make me look like an indifferent and self-absorbed bastard.

I held my thoughts since I didn't know where her own dislike for that group was coming from.

Mine was partly because I didn't understand the depth of their moral authority, the immutable certainty with which they said things about the 'post-colonial world' of which they were clearly the true voices. I'd heard more about that 'post-colonial world' in a few days than all the years I lived in it, breathed its air, smelled its filth, lost my virginity in one of its many dark underbellies, survived years of crushing depression in its hold, endured its psychosis in the fragmented lives of my parents and their friends who crossed European ideas with anything they could find in their local milieu. But *that* 'post-colonial world', which I apparently 'embodied', was nothing like the fully formed and footnoted gunfire sentences I heard from Sara Chakraborty, nothing like the costumed performances of the Ugandan writer. Mine was just another tired world of ordinary and complicated people trudging along, like anywhere else, mostly oblivious of life beyond their neighbourhood, full of pain or courting happiness, vile or honest.

Perky's presence was refreshing because it was new and held the possibility of an exit towards a different picture of America. I believed this more strongly when she offered me a cigarette and lit it for me. And while I smoked that first stick in America she sketched a portrait of a life that reminded me of the books I'd read, bringing some warmth to my heart, lifting me from the depths of 'post-colonial despair' to a place where, for a second, it seemed like I was now entering my true idea of America.

As 'a working-class chick from Ohio' who grew up with a single 'drug-addicted mother' in a 'trailer park' she could 'sniff BS from a mile away'.

It wasn't the sniffing that I liked but the little biographical detail, the image it conjured of the mother sitting on a foldable chair outside her trailer, smoking a joint or whatever she was addicted to, her enormous breasts pouring out of her distended tank top, and little Perky in whatever space was designated for her in the trailer, playing with some Barbie doll or dreaming of a faraway land, of an escape from the backward flatness of her small town to San Francisco or New York.

A smile crossed my face when she mentioned her actual escape from her hometown at the age of seventeen, driving east to New York for college at Vassar, after which she lived for two years in the Catskills, in 'a community of makers and seekers' from all over, and it was there that she met her first husband, a black poet from Damascus, Virginia, who had fled an abusive family to 'just live and thrive' up north.

I pictured some kind of twenty-first-century underground railroad where black folks were fleeing north or wherever to 'live and thrive'.

When the 'community' disintegrated, after it came out that the 'leader' kept 'crossing the boundaries', she and the black poet moved to Lisbon for a year, travelling around Europe. They separated in Rome, after an 'incident', and she came back to the States, where she applied and got the job at William Blake.

The job itself was disappointing when it did not deliver what she needed to 'thrive'. But she knew 'this year would be different' when she read my email and looked me up.

I pinched the cigarette butt harder than necessary.

A group of students walked past.

I tried to make sense of the gaps in her story, the omissions and vagueness.

When she said she had read my book, I not only tensed but also understood clearly why she was sharing her 'journey' with me. She saw similarities between some aspects of her life and that of my character, and she could also tell that I was 'more daring and original' than the other fellows.

I wasn't sure about the originality but I was flattered all the same, and she compared my work to 'something Salinger would have written if he was born and raised in Africa'.

I felt a rush of blood and a little warmth in my crotch. It was a new feeling, this positive response to a compliment from a reader of my work. Maybe it was the atmosphere, sitting on that bench in a dreamy spot on a quiet campus in America. Maybe a part of me was craving reassurance, some form of acceptance. I suddenly felt proud of my work, its universal appeal, its ability to gather the human condition far and near under its own relatable roof.

Out of curiosity, I asked how she got my book.

Apparently, Betty had donated her copy to the Harry Putnam Library and Perky had borrowed it soon after I sent her my initial inquiry. She had repeated those words, 'initial inquiry', which made me wonder if she still remembered the typo in my email, 'the global dementias of violent hosieries'. My mood swung from where it was to a lower rung.

Involuntarily, I looked at Comstock Place, hoping to find an excuse to flee the scene.

She uncrossed her legs, as if to reorder my gaze.

She tugged the edges of her skirt.

She asked me, 'How about we take this conversation elsewhere?'

She stood up and I found myself following her, my mind suspended between confidence and crushing self-doubt. I didn't care to ask where we were going. There was an air of command and authority about her that magnetised me. And she seemed to know this about herself and her voice, because she did not wait for me to answer or look to see if I was comfortable following her. She simply led and I followed like a loyal dog. She had also, in that instant, transformed from the 'sharing' Perky to a more dominant figure who knew precisely what she wanted, and how and where she wanted it.

As we walked towards the gate, away from the vicinities of Comstock Place, she took a small bottle from her handbag and sipped. 'Care for some?' she asked.

I accepted and was glad I did. It was whisky and it tasted like nothing I knew from life back home. I studied the bottle and the label said something about the Hudson Valley.

She pointed to a narrow road to our left, just before the gate.

I saw a sign saying it led to one of the campus car parks. I followed her again. And I took in for the first time her height and shape, how tall she was, a foot or more above me, slightly hunched. How old was she? I tried to guess but concluded it did not matter. If she wasn't my age she was at most thirty-five. But it didn't matter. There was something in the air, in that moment, that had seized me by the collar and was dragging me along, and I felt the move itself was a walk into a different and more intriguing world.

By the time we reached her car, a black Subaru Forester, and after my third swig from her bottle, I was beginning to sense a long and exciting night ahead. She exuded the energy of a host leading a guest to the sanctum sanctorum of a crowded party, away from the crowd, towards a more exclusive offering. I tried to imagine where she was taking me but quickly resisted the urge to dwell in fantasy.

When she said something about having a better drink back at her place my head spun in multiple directions. Now I gave my mind free rein, conjuring all sorts of images as she reversed the car and drove away.

It took us a little over twenty minutes to reach her place, a period of time we spent trading what we despised about the likes of Sara and Kabumba. I felt understood and accepted chatting with her. By the time we entered her house, we were already brushing against each other's bodies, hovering close enough that kisses came naturally, her lips enclosing mine, and I felt the strength of her tongue, its probing powers, and a part of me wondered if Kabumba would ever experience this aspect of America, this other type of welcome.

We stumbled deeper and deeper into her large living room, which was mostly empty and dimly lit. We landed on her couch, the only thing of substance that I saw.

As if recalling an appointment, she sprang up and commanded me to come with her. She pulled me up and I followed, self-consciously dragging my hard-on with me.

At the door to her bedroom, she asked me to close my eyes, turn around, and wait. 'You'll like what you're about to see,' she said. She went in and I stood there, trying to process what was happening and how fast it was unfolding. There was anticipation but also a hovering awareness that something was off. She had mentioned that she lived alone in the Stonehill part of town, which she described, or rather dismissed, as 'a little sleepy but nice', and I imagined a small flat, not a multi-room mini-mansion set back from the street. It wasn't clear if she owned or rented but these details didn't matter and I was not interested in asking, at least not in that moment of anticipation.

I could hear her moving inside, and could hear the music coming on, a piece that sounded familiar, like it was rising from deep inside a part of me that was long dead or repressed. And when she called out for me to turn and see, I saw a scene that simultaneously impressed and embarrassed me. The candles were there, along with enlarged pictures on the walls, and the music came back to me, the same 'Sweet Georgia Brown' I'd played and liked and thrown into a scene in my novel. She had recreated that scene, bringing the imagination of my young protagonist to life in her large bedroom. She'd planned it all and was waiting for the right time to 'invite me over' and how 'perfect' that it 'worked out' the way it did.

I looked around and saw the scene again as it appeared in my book, awkwardly thrown in after I'd googled names and places to make it all sound real. My young protagonist had read the now out-of-print *Midnight Orgies* by the Swiss-American writer Jean Rudolph Lauper, and had imagined himself in one of Lauper's orgies in Greenwich Village in the early twentieth century, receiving a blowjob from a flamboyant 'queen', surrounded by portraits of 'well-known Bohemians' on the wall, 'their faces barely illuminated by low-burning candles placed at different corners'. His anachronism was mine, born out of a period when I fancied myself a 'bohemian', enamoured by distant and faded worlds. I was a curious creature formed by the stories I heard from my parents and their friends, by the things I read.

As I entered the room I understood one could simultaneously have a hard-on while cringing and praying for one's embarrassing past to disappear.

She had stripped down to a glittering bra and a black thong, just as my character described the 'lady that threw herself at me while the queen sucked my dick'.

Now it seemed Perky was making my book into a movie, with major twists that I couldn't help but notice. The posters on the walls weren't the ones in my book. Hers were of black intellectuals and writers and activists and celebrities. Baldwin, Fanon, Idris Elba, Angela Davis, Oprah. I tried to speak and she put a finger to her lips, like the Greenwich Village 'lady' in my book. She descended on me, straddled me and undressed me so fast I could barely recall when the grinding began and when I started squeezing her arse with equal intensity. She lifted herself and disappeared again and when she returned she had ropes and a big bottle of champagne. This too I recalled from the scene in my book. The champagne was coming down my mouth in no time, my legs and arms tied to the bedposts and her on top of me. The music shuffled from one twenties jazz to another, louder this time. The audience on the wall seemed to come alive, as my young character had imagined. Now it was Baldwin and Idris Elba, visible on the left wall, that looked on as Perky – naked by this time – continued to grind, the champagne bottle placed on the side table. She left again and returned with something in her mouth, which she offered me in a kiss, a pill, like the 'lady' had done in my book. I asked what it was and she said, 'It's nothing,' and I was already too drunk to resist. I actually did not want to resist and did not care because for the first time in my life someone was taking the time and pain to create something special for me no matter how absurd it was. Whatever concerns I had vanished when she turned and sat on my face.

Between the rush of that unknown pill and the phenomenal sensation of the face-sitting, what followed simultaneously erased itself as it unfolded.

I recall bits and pieces and vaguely remember her disappearing and reappearing with a black mask and a giant afro, and I recall laughing as she said something about showing me how she 'truly' saw herself, 'like that bitch over there,' she said, pointing at a figure that could have been either Angela Davis or Oprah. I kept laughing disproportionately as she rode me and slapped my cheeks so hard I felt it in my brain.

She'd gone off-script from the scene in my book and there was no going back. I vaguely recall how she raised her fist as she came, and after that it was the blankness of night.

It was this experience that inspired one of my lectures at the Global Centre for Gender and Equality at the Osakwe University of Southern Nigeria.

In that lecture, titled 'Diasporic Erotics: Inter/course as New World Dialogic Dis-course', I relied on a 'combination of first-hand encounters and a sustained body of lucidly researched ideas' to argue that 'the future of our planet, from the realisation of gender equality to the end of racism and the clearing out of all anxieties produced by the excesses of the modern world, not to forget the horrors of late capitalism and the rapid and riotous and raucous resurgence of ferocious fascist fetishisms' depended on 'a carefully orchestrated indulgence of bodily proximities'. I argued further that the 'flowering of bodily proximities across geo-temporal itineraries could potentially do more for global cultural understanding than all the Peace Corps and Fulbright and NGO-esque pre- and post-Cold War simulations and vigorous insistence on difference'. I recall lifting my head to see if someone would interrupt me with a question but no one did and I was grateful because I had no idea what I was saying. During the short break a young scholar about my age came close to me and asked if I could share a thing or two about the 'widening rift' between the political sides in the US. I nodded solemnly as if giving serious thought to his question, threw some cashew nuts into my mouth, munched contemplatively, formulating my answer as the bespectacled young scholar in his oversized and outdated suit and skinny necktie waited patiently in the overpowering heat. Unsure what to say, I spoke through a smirk, noting that he should never take that 'widening rift' seriously. Lowering my voice, I told him that enduring and observing politics in the US 'is the same as having your arse cheeks held apart while a unicorn rams its horn up your behind, the Left holding your left cheek and the Right holding the right and both sides taking delight in watching their unicorn doing justice to your arse'. I threw in more cashew nuts and returned to the rostrum, leaving him to meditate on my spur-of-the-moment advice. It was at this same lecture that I mentioned the 'fact' that the burgeoning pornography industry in Nigeria and Africa as a whole 'is a sign of radical progress' and a true break from 'the primitive conservatism that shackles the present to the primordial past'. The success of that lecture led to a well-paid invitation to give a talk on 'new positions for global harmony' at the Nigerian Institute of World Relations, and I thanked that night in Perky's bed for the inspiration.

I remember waking up the next morning around ten, my head pounding, the room transformed to an ordinary space without the costumes and the posters, its dark grey walls so blank and boring I wondered if I had dreamed the previous night.

Perky wasn't there. She'd left a note to let me know she was off to Concord to 'co-lead' an outreach programme that introduced minorities to the 'great outdoors'.

There was bread and eggs and bacon and I was told to please make myself breakfast.

I checked my phone and saw a text she sent at 8 a.m. to say she'd arrived and the activities were going great, with a selfie of herself standing in the centre of knee-high pillars marking 'the original location of Thoreau's cabin'.

I took a hot shower and made myself scrambled eggs and toast and avoided the bacon. She'd asked if I could wait to have lunch at a place she liked downtown but I decided I needed to re-enter the world alone.

10

'IT'S amazing what you can accomplish in four months if you're passionate enough to put in the work.' The room full of aspiring Nigerian writers nodded and some took notes. I was leading the first Chief F.K.J. Igbikhedia Fellowship for Writers of Immense Promise. The location: a quiet resort tucked away in the Obudu Plateau in Cross River State in southern Nigeria. The seven-day programme, comprising 'workshops and seminars on craft', was conceived by my agent slash publisher as the African version of the William Blake Fellowship, sold to the writing community as 'a fully funded opportunity to encourage aesthetic and stylistic diversity in contemporary creative-critical writing', and we encouraged applications from 'writers who tackle social issues'. Hundreds of applications flooded in, from Fez in Morocco to L'Agulhas in South Africa. From this diverse pool we selected ten African writers from Nigeria. I led the workshops while my publisher led the 'seminars on craft'. And each morning, before the sessions began, I would sit outside my cabin, one of many scattered on the side of the plateau overlooking the eastern view of the mountain range, and sip my coffee, taking in the silence of nature, away from Port Jumbo. I enjoyed these quiet moments and preferred them to the workshops and the company of my students. Their interest in the publishing 'markets' of Europe and America, and their endless chattering about this and that 'lit mag' that accepted or rejected their 'work' in London and New York and Sydney, and that grant they got or didn't get from so-and-so organisation in Santa Fe and Marfa and Berlin and everywhere but Nigeria drained me. From their modest homes in Nigeria, starved of support for their work and talent, they looked outwards for opportunities, their abilities and stories and energies thrown about to any organisation and programme that offered support. Not once did I hear them discussing the motives behind the generous grants and fellowships and residencies they pursued, or pause to ponder where and how the funds were raised. If it paid, and if it helped them escape the horrors of daily life in Nigeria, they went for it. Listening to them, I thought to myself that the days of sending secret agents as field workers to scout for ideas in remote Africa were over; a single contest for African writers organised from London or New York or Paris or Moscow or Beijing could bring the best and brightest to you on a platter. In the past you had to plant your agents on the ground, as professors or writers or journalists, to do the legwork; all you needed now was a wealthy individual as your front, a prize or fellowship named after them, a clever mission statement, a reputable and diverse panel of judges, a call for submission, and the world of African ideas would come rushing to your doorstep. A contest organised for less than $50,000 could fetch enough ideas to enrich your foreign and socio-economic policies, yielding millions if not billions of dollars in indirect benefits. And the prize money could potentially be recovered by way of submission fees paid by the desperate applicants.

My agent took advantage of that pool of desperate voices. He understood the politics and economics of literary prizes, having himself spent years entering what he described as 'my wretched poems' for contests around the world, collecting rejections while losing money.

Bitter, disillusioned and aware that the odds were stacked against 'the writers now emerging in Africa', he reached out to Chief F.K.J. Igbikhedia, a reclusive millionaire whose reclusion was not unconnected to his dealings with warlords in various civil wars across Africa.

The chief had already collaborated with a couple of top professors to set up the Centre for Advanced Studies, where bright scientists from across the country were offered funding simply to think and theorise and present their work to the general public.

We had direct access to the chief, thanks to an old friend of my father's, a professor of theoretical physics at the Tropical School of Technology, who now directed the chief's Centre for Advanced Studies.

'A Princeton man', as he was known to my father's circle, the professor read my agent's proposal, thought it was 'clever' and 'exactly what we needed now to advance a robust cultural front in this age of liquid change'.

A week later we received an invitation from the chief's secretary. They flew us first class to Abuja, where the chief resided in an exclusive section of the nation's capital.

The 'meeting' took place at a social gathering the chief had organised for his friends and 'associates', and it was obvious that we were there as the cultural arm of his empire.

He engaged us for two minutes or less, during which he made two quick remarks – 'My secretary will make all the necessary arrangements' and 'Please don't forget to give her your account numbers' – before he disappeared into the large banquet room of the Southern Ritz Hotel, which was teeming with his business partners and investors and senior employees from around the world, including a number of Nollywood celebrities.

The moment of encounter with the chief was anti-climactic for Belema. Deep down he expected the chief to show signs of genuine interest in culture, to throw in a line or two about the project. The disappointment evolved into a long night of him trying to drum up a moral justification for the project he had proposed. At least the writers we would end up working with wouldn't have to hawk their identities or play up any narrative to secure money to write. Besides, he was doing what others had done elsewhere, recycling and laundering 'wealth' to build 'our own culture'. And that was how 'the West arrived where they are now, culturally speaking, the museums and historic mansions and botanical gardens and cathedrals and whole cities'. We're just following their footsteps, 'and don't let them preach all that moral crap, we can do the moral thing when we've reached where they are. How else are we going to fund the arts here?'

I understood his point but wondered out loud if he thought the world unfolded on a straight line and at different rates for different regions and we were somehow trapped in the past and slowly crawling to meet those ahead.

He looked at me like someone watching an actor losing his marbles on stage. I was already too involved to play the moral intellectual, and I felt the bite of guilt for challenging him the way I did.

It was past midnight in the nation's capital. We were sitting on the wide balcony of our hotel, on the tenth floor, and we could see the movement of lights on the network of streets stretching into the distance. 'I would like to visit the outskirts,' I said, changing the subject. The slums and semi-slums had sprung up after Abuja emerged from nowhere and became the capital in the nineties, uprooting and displacing the communities that lived there, pushing them away to fend for themselves in the outskirts of a city that continued to expand with little regard for the social amenities that sustained modern cities.

'We all need our share of slum tourism and poverty porn,' he said, his words slurred, a sarcastic smile on his face. 'I guess you also picked that up from the US, eh? Ogling the poor to conceal your own poverty, looking over your shoulder to see how bad they have it over there while you bleed from the inside. Well, if you're looking for me tomorrow I'll be touring the site of the new Universal City.'

His love for this new 'ultramodern' city within the Federal Capital Territory, still under construction, was another extension of his disillusion. Since abandoning political poetry, he'd embraced everything that reeked of 'modernisation', a sign that 'we' were making progress like 'the rest of the world'.

I stood up, grabbed the nearly empty bottle of whisky and retired to my room.

I left him because the subject was reeling back a chain of memories in Boston. His mood and remarks triggered me the same way his encounter with the chief affected him. I was feeling again my sense of powerlessness in Boston, the combined feeling of gratitude and wanting to assert my freedom as an individual, a feeling that came into full intensity when I visited the Kirkpatricks for dinner at their home in Scotsbury, outside Boston, a place they'd recently moved to after many years in Charlestown. Betty had suggested that I could stay the night if I wanted, and I agreed.

When I emerged from the station that day, my satchel flung across my shoulder, bulging with the items I needed for the night, I saw Betty waiting for me by a black SUV. When I approached, she clasped me in a tight and unexpected hug that nearly cut off my circulation. I could sense the pride in her warm embrace. The writer and his patron. 'I can't believe you're here,' she said. Neither can I, I wanted to say, but instead I mumbled something incoherent and sustained a smile.

As she drove away from the train station, towards our destination, we passed large houses, mostly in shades of blue and grey. The ocean bordered the houses to the left, separated from the road by rocks and beach sand. The coastline, spreading out on one side and disappearing into the distance, blurred into the grey horizon of the bay.

We crossed a bridge over the North River, and I saw its dark shape winding its way to the bay, giving of itself to the ocean, like the River Niger back home.

'And how are you settling in?' she asked.

'So far so good,' I replied, hoping I'd not betrayed the truth lurking in my heart, that so far I'd not managed to connect with anyone on the programme. I didn't think I should mention Perky, as that might lead to a suspicion of staff–fellow intimacy.

We slowed down and turned onto a dirt road.

She was now asking about my first impressions, but my attention was on a deer I'd spotted ahead which, startled by the approaching car, had jumped into the bushes. I peeled my eyes to that side of the road, hoping to spot it again.

'It couldn't be more different from Port Jumbo,' I finally replied.

She was happy, she was now saying, to see me 'here in the States'.

The dean wasn't there when we arrived. He was out on some errand.

She showed me my room, a large space that was twice the size of my room back home. From the window I could see a wooden pier and a small inlet of the ocean.

On the bedside table, I saw that she'd carefully stacked three books: *Beloved* by Toni Morrison, *No Longer at Ease* by Chinua Achebe and *The Final Passage* by Caryl Phillips.

Hanging on the wall, at the head of the bed, was a painting of a lighthouse, which I instantly recognised as the Port Jumbo lighthouse, made famous by Mary Browne, the British artist who painted it from six different angles, all versions ending up in museums around the world. But I could tell that the one on the wall was painted by a local Port Jumbo artist. This was confirmed when I drew closer and saw the signature,

Tamunorex, and in my mind I could see this particular painter's studio on the eastern promenade.

On the other bedside table I saw a magazine. I went closer. On the glossy cover was a group photo of elegantly dressed black men and women, in black suits and white shirts, and it said they were the major black writers one must read. I studied their faces, the opulent background against which they stood, and wondered where I fit in, and why she'd placed the magazine there (obviously because of me, but why?). I was failing to draw inspiration from that image.

During the pre-dinner drinks, I found myself sandwiched on one side by the Kirkpatricks and on the other by Dr Kathryn B. Reinhardt and her husband, Professor George Reinhardt. The Reinhardts had driven down from Boston. I hadn't been aware that they were joining us. We were all in the living room, by the electric fireplace. Through the sliding glass door, the pier and the houses across the inlet were visible. The conversation somehow stayed on the weather, how the last winter had lingered longer than the previous one. Betty occasionally dropped lines about the weather in Africa, and they would all pause and look in my direction. Someone else would jump in and continue the conversation.

I excused myself and went to the bathroom.

I needed space to work myself into a conversational mood, to feel as lively as they were.

I flashed my teeth in the mirror and held the pose until my cheeks hurt.

I rolled my shoulders.

I opened my eyes until my eyelids couldn't take it.

I slapped myself on both cheeks.

When I returned, there were more guests, a middle-aged woman and her teenage daughter who, as Betty said, had recently returned from a group trip to India, where she and the others from their high school had volunteered at 'a school for Dalit children'. She was now interested in Africa after a refugee from Kibera, presently living in the US, visited their school last fall to share his experience of growing up in that Kenyan slum.

I had read about Kibera, and knew it was one of the largest slums in the world, one hell of an eyesore, a depressing fact that wasn't obvious in the high schooler's voice. What I heard instead was a load of enthusiasm and excitement at the prospect of travelling there. I admired her interest, in spite of my personal feelings.

I excused myself again and hurried to the bathroom.

I returned and my first attempt to be lively was a disaster. My voice was shrill and loud.

The Reinhardts squinted. The Kirkpatricks winced. The high-school Africanist and her mother kept their broad smile, as if to counterbalance the look of suspicion coming from the others.

I was talking about the dry season in Nigeria, how different it was from winter, no snow and all that, a topic Betty had raised while I was in the bathroom, and on which I felt obliged to offer further context, an authentic angle.

I gesticulated a little too much and my wine glass flew out of my hand, shattering at the feet of the dean, its red contents dousing his white socks and making a Basquiat-esque splash on the floor.

The silence that descended was as profound as it was unsettling. Not a word. Just my voice apologising. My hands shaking.

Betty leaped into action, cleaning up the mess before I could do so. She patted my shoulder, and said, 'It happens all the time. We've all been there.'

They laughed. I tried to laugh but I thought I heard something else in Betty's voice, in their collective laughter.

As if to show how conversations were made, Kathryn began to share her 'journey' to William Blake, in response to a question on how to work in the 'field of ethnic studies' posed by the young Africanist. Kathryn took us back to Riverville, Wisconsin, where she was born and raised. She was the first to go to college, where she read English with a focus on African American and Native American Studies at the University of Madison, after which she moved to Boston for a postdoc at Boylston Graduate School. After her postdoc, she joined William Blake as an adjunct, teaching classes in ethnic studies, and eventually 'transitioned' to a full-time post. She continued her story while I agonised over the wine glass incident, praying for the evening to hurry up and end.

When we transferred to the table, the dean sat at one end and Betty at the other. The Reinhardts were on one side, opposite me. The high-school Africanist sat to the left of the Reinhardts, facing me, her mother to my right, facing her.

Behind the Reinhardts, a horrible oil painting hung in full glare, clearly a purchase by Betty from one of her visits to Nigeria. The painting showed a canoe on a beach, with abandoned nets and jerrycans on both sides.

I caught the dean's thick signet ring glittering on his left little finger, and saw how the collar of his sea-blue shirt hung like a sea holly above his grey V-neck sweater.

George Reinhardt was a fascinating presence. He seldom spoke. And hardly smiled. His thin hair lay like a circular silk bandage around his bald head. A visibly ascetic man, he communicated by moving his eyes and letting them fall on yours, and somehow you intuitively knew what he was thinking. For instance, when his wife used a rather warm conversation about Roxane Gay – whose work she loved and had included in her syllabus – as a segue into a speech on the dearth of diverse voices in classrooms and academia in general, saying this more for my benefit since the subject wasn't new among those present, George lifted his eyes, held them until they lowered and found mine, and his message came across in a slight rolling of the eyes that seemed to say, 'Well, how about you give up your position as the director of ethnic studies and make room for a qualified person of colour.' He came across as the type who would either take action or simply enjoy whatever privileges the system offered him. He'd spent his entire life in New England and bore his insulation with stoic pride. He seemed to know exactly who he was, what he represented, and did not pretend to care about the things he didn't truly care about. He simply existed where he was, a figure grounded in the routine and tedium of academia, cocooned by the privileges of existing in a world designed to favour him. His wife, on the other hand, fluttered with what I could only see as either extreme guilt or a projection of unresolved anxiety. I was beginning to lose count of the number of times she'd said 'white people' in mock despair or just to emphasise a point. When George, in his only chatty moment, mentioned his ice fishing weekends in the Berkshires, a subject I thought was refreshing and enlightening, Kathryn destroyed the mood with her remark, 'Ugh, white people stuff.' She swerved the conversation and began talking about the issue of 'safe spaces' for students, how her programme was working hard to secure more funding for minorities, how they were making sure students from less privileged backgrounds, especially 'people of colour', were given equal opportunities. I listened, knowing it was all meant for me to see and understand that *they* were the good guys, that *I* was safe at William Blake, safe around her and everyone at that table – a gesture that was in reality having the opposite effect on me, since I was now beginning to imagine the possibility of hostilities everywhere outside that circle.

Breaking the theme, the dean asked what my first impressions were.

'First impressions?' I repeated. 'Well, I think the absence of chaos is striking. I mean, compared to where I'm from. Here, there are no motorbikes and cars blaring their horns, no bars playing loud music at every street corner, no street hawkers with megaphones screaming at you their invitations to buy magic soaps and antimalarial tree roots.' I wanted to say something about the Comstock protest but didn't.

My reply, for some season, drew silence. I felt they were waiting for more, for a sustained talk on my 'experience' in America. I panicked. Disconcerted, I poured myself another glass of wine, and from the corner of my eye I caught Kathryn squinting at my full glass. 'You must be looking forward to meeting our students,' she said, 'they're excited about this cohort of William Blake Fellows.'

She was fascinated by my proposed work on George Thompson, she added, and was interested in my 'transatlantic roots' and the 'global histories' captured in my 'work'.

She was quoting me here, pulling from my application statement, nudging me to talk. She must have read the 'initial inquiry' that I sent Perky, and the 'global histories' probably came from my 'global dementias of violent hosieries'. I prayed for a hatch to open underneath my chair. My only option was to ignore her comments. And when I didn't take the bait, she wondered – not to me in particular – if there was a way to have 'this year's fellows write up their talks, that way we could put together a little book'. Wouldn't that be a good idea?

George nodded and forked his asparagus.

I drank my wine a little too fast.

The dean rotated the ring on his finger.

The high-school Africanist, who seemed to consume me with her eyes instead of eating her food, reached for her glass of water. The evening dragged on. I retreated into myself, burdened by a growing feeling that I wasn't representing as I should.

For a second I wished I had the guts and liveliness of Kabumba and the astuteness and rhetorical prowess of Sara Chakraborty. They would have turned the evening into a theatre of publishable ideas and memorable anecdotes, and there would have been laughter and tears and the sort of catharsis Americans seem to expect when the oppressed and the oppressor dine together.

I wasn't delivering the goods and wasn't keeping my side of the bargain; the sense of balance that they were accustomed to having at occasions like that wasn't being achieved.

I thought of the room Betty had prepared for me, with Morrison and Achebe and Phillips on one side, and a host of black writers on the other, and suddenly a well of anger sprang up inside me, which I fought to conceal.

When the would-be Africanist, eyes glittering with anticipation, asked what it was like 'growing up in Africa', I tried to advance a simple one-liner, something to simultaneously answer but also evade. But Betty, eager to show her knowledge, launched into her experience of teaching kids in East Africa as a Peace Corps volunteer. It wasn't the accuracy or inaccuracy of her intervention that set me off. It was the way she spoke as though her East African experience, in the seventies, applied to every single village and town and city on the continent, across time periods and languages and cultures shaped by different traditional and colonial experiences.

My reaction was incoherent and impassioned, forced through a combination of caution, confusion, respect and repulsion, and the result was everything from how the forces that shaped the modern world, transforming the disparate European groups at that dinner table into Americans, were also responsible for turning the average city dweller in Africa into a hybrid creature whose life is split between the multiple influences and traditions going back to the same period that Europe began making its inroads in what would eventually become the United States. I staggered back to the Romans in northern Africa, to early Christian settlements in that region, jumped to the Portuguese and Dutch and English in southern Africa, and the worlds of trade and culture and violence that shaped identities down there and everywhere. I rambled on, cheered by the wine, cheered by the desire to break free and plant myself outside what seemed a cage of received and glamourised and unquestioned ideas, cheered by my own insecurities and inability to just play along.

And somewhere in my spontaneous lecture, I feared there was something truly wrong with me, an irreparable flaw, a gap in my thinking and being; I feared they all had access to some pure and morally correct knowledge that I did not.

I longed to summarise with one of those terse and tweetable lines you hear from some writers of the 'immigrant experience' who seemed to know how to lambast white audiences without losing their support, a tactic Sara Chakraborty once described as 'postcolonial proximity to privilege as resistance'. I wanted them to know that I wasn't advancing any single ideology or worldview or notion of progress, and wasn't trying to attack anyone, that I just wanted to exist and cry and laugh and fuck and live and die without prefixing or suffixing my actions with any universal idea of blackness or Africanness or whatever thing out there that I was supposedly tied to as a POC or BAME.

Betty rose and started clearing the dishes. They all joined her, moving in different directions.

They congregated near the kitchen. I sat where I was, alone at the dinner table, composing a text to Perky.

I could hear the young Africanist chatting with George, sharing stories of her ski adventures the previous winter. Kathryn and the dean stood to one side, talking in low voices. Betty and Lauren, the high schooler's mother, stood by the kitchen counter, talking about their volunteer work at a homeless shelter in the next town.

When it was time for the Reinhardts to leave, I saw my opportunity to head back to Boston. Perky had replied to my text asking if I could stay the night at her place. Better to endure her clamps on my nipples than bear a night in the room Betty had prepared for me.

The Reinhardts dropped me off at the station downtown. I took a train to Stonehill. On the train, I tried to suppress my experience at the Kirkpatricks but it was impossible to do so. I caught myself looking at my own black fingers where they rested on my knees, and glancing sideways to catch a glimpse of the white faces around me. I looked around to see if there were other black people in the carriage. I spotted a black teenager and stared at him until he caught me staring and changed his seat.

Out on Kendell Avenue, I stopped at a liquor store run by a bespectacled man who I overheard saying to a customer that his parents 'moved here from Las Piedras' in Puerto Rico.

I wandered around the store and eventually settled for a pack of Sam Adams.

At the till, the man from Las Piedras asked for my ID.

I showed him my Nigerian driver's licence. He held it up, looked at me then back at the ID, and asked, 'Any American ID?'

'No,' I answered, and told him that I was new in the US.

Something sparked in his eyes. I couldn't tell what it was but it was warm and understanding.

'Well,' he said, 'welcome to the United States of America.'

He returned my driver's licence.

Turning around, I saw those in line behind me: two black men, each holding a bottle of hard liquor, and a sad-looking white woman in grey sweatpants hugging a large bottle of vodka. They were all staring at me, the new creature from Africa.

Hurrying out the door, I began the walk to Perky's nice neighbourhood, away from the area around the liquor store, which seemed like the threshold between two sides of the socio-economic divide. Perky had offered to pick me up but I wanted to walk off my anxiety.

A minute or so into my walk, I stood and opened a can of beer.

There were two cans left when I got to Perky's.

11

My second and humiliating outburst in Boston involved Kabumba, who had taken it upon himself to chastise me for not 'producing work'. I could tell that he was truly disappointed. He was the sort of writer who saw himself as the carrier of his continent's honour, the defender of 'his people' against all forms of misconceptions. His capacity to simultaneously charm his audience while defending his dear continent was astonishing. If he saw Africa as his to protect, insisting on the need for 'African writers' to produce 'authentic' stories, Sara was in charge of the post-colonial world, calling on her intimidating repertoire of theoretical insights to 'contextualise' the 'legacies of colonial encounters and ruptures'. She 'situated' my 'post-colonial refusal to write in the long histories of' something or other that I quickly forgot because it gave me an instant migraine. Deepak, the Nepali writer, was indifferent and did not take it upon himself to drag me for not producing work. Claudia González did not care either. She thought I was charming, that I carried the aura of writers who became famous for the 'precise fact' that they stopped writing or wrote so infrequently that every word was eagerly awaited. She called me an 'artist of silence', a writer 'dwelling in a space of silence', like 'Rimbaud who refused to write', and suggested I read *Bartleby & Co* by Enrique Vila-Matas. She made these remarks while we were sitting outside Café Pamplona in Harvard Square, with Deepak, Kabumba and Sara. We were months into our residency and they'd each had two public readings, submitted three pieces of work, and led several workshops for undergraduates. I hadn't done any, providing Kabumba with a generous opportunity to be disappointed in his fellow African writer. He and I reported to the same supervisor, one Professor of the Practice of Prose and author of *Feathers of Conscience* (Honeysuckle Press, 1980), a one-hit wonder that secured the writer several fellowships to travel through Europe in the late eighties and early nineties. I had a feeling the Professor of the Practice of Prose, or PoPoP, and Kabumba discussed me behind my back. I was sure they did, in fact, since Kabumba once asked, 'Frank, is it true you haven't been submitting work?', following this with another question: 'Why's your name absent from the seminar roster? I thought we were all supposed to give talks?' After that he stopped talking to me, except in moments when he saw an opportunity to make sweeping pronouncements intended to put me in my place while defending Africanness. For example, his response to Claudia González's remark that day at Café Pamplona was a direct attack: 'A writer writes, and for us African writers we must write to correct centuries of colonial misrepresentations. It is our duty to confront narrow-minded accounts of Africa. We must make it clear that Africa is not a country.' I tried to reply but he fired on. 'Until the lion learns to speak, the tale will always be the hunter's.' Deepak was nodding at this remark while texting on his phone. I thought hard about what he was saying. I contemplated an answer but dismissed the whole thing. Instead I looked straight ahead and kept my eyes on a group of Chinese tourists taking selfies in front of the Church of St Paul.

That same week, I was standing outside Café Roma on Pratt Street sharing a joint with a homeless man I'd come to know when I saw Kabumba with a group of other Africans holding up placards protesting the arrest of some journalist slash activist slash NGO worker in faraway Angola. I'll never forget how they looked at me, shook their heads and marched on. And with them that day was some Nigerian chap I had met at a conference on 'Growth and Opportunities in Africa', organised by William Blake in collaboration with the Institute of African Studies at nearby Roxbury University. The young man had delivered a paper on 'Nigeria and Its Centrality to Africa's Rising Markets' and his presentation was so fantastic that I applauded at the end. He'd pointed out the 'strategic location of Nigeria on the map of Africa', how Nigeria was 'positioned as a trigger' on the map. 'See,' he said, pointing at a blank map of Africa with the spot for Nigeria highlighted in green, 'see how Africa is shaped as a pistol pointing down-wards?' And indeed, we all saw that, and quickly saw how Nigeria was in fact the 'trigger' of that pistol. 'Any growth in Nigeria,' he said, shooting his audience a very African smile, 'triggers growth around the continent.' I found myself itching to chat with him afterwards. There he was with a group of fellow presenters, Nigerian Ivy Leaguers. I approached them, aware that I reeked of tobacco, my forest of a beard contrasting with their clean-shaven faces. I was also aware that I wasn't schooled in the lingo of Africans educated in Europe and America, their savvy cosmopolitanspeak. I just wanted to tell the chap what I thought of his presentation, that I liked the metaphor, that it must have made a lot of sense to Americans who truly knew about guns. But as I approached, their body language made it clear that they didn't want to be associated with this unkempt creature. It was there on their faces, on their drawn lips. Wounded, I shelved my compliment. I broke into their circle, stretched out my hand to the chap for a handshake, and attacked him with the first thing that came to my mind. 'That was a nice metaphor,' I said, 'but I wonder if a penis would have made a better metaphor. You see, Africa does look like a large penis pointing downwards, with South Africa as the very tip, and West Africa as the scrotum, which puts Nigeria somewhere at the intersection of the barrel and the nut sack.' I left them to digest my comment, grinning as I grabbed a handful of mints from a tray near the exit.

It was on the walk back to campus, after seeing Kabumba and his fellow protesters, that I saw an old but still working typewriter left on the side of the street. I picked it up and called it Dos Passos. I wasn't sure why I named it after that American writer. Maybe it was something the homeless man had said about wanting to be somewhere in the world where he could actually write the 'United States of America' on a 'postcard' and send it home, which made me think of Dos Passos and the line about 'USA' as 'the letters at the end of an address when you are away from home'. And maybe it was the weed, a strain my homeless buddy said would 'get me going', or maybe I was subconsciously trying to prove Kabumba wrong, but I saw in that old typewriter my opportunity to break free from my anxieties and write.

I carried it off to my room and the next day I bought the right paper and ribbon and got a big bottle of cheap whisky. And that night, as Glenn Miller played on Spotify, I recreated a scene from a black and white movie I once saw about a reclusive writer in New York struggling to complete the novel that would later make him famous. It was the sixties again and I was living that writer's life. I could see him hunched over his desk, his drink to one side and his typewriter in front of him.

I cranked the music up and drank and typed away and dreamed.

At some point, feeling confident, I stepped back from my desk and took pictures of the scene and texted them to Perky, and she replied to ask if I wanted to 'take the party' to her place. I ignored her text and re-downloaded Instagram and logged into the account I had created a year before but abandoned. I resized one picture and posted it, and for some reason I decided to spy on Sara Chakraborty's and Kabumba's pages.

Kabumba's was predictable: photos of African landscapes and pictures of himself at important literary functions. Sara's was the complete opposite of what I expected. I'd seen her Twitter page and knew she tweeted and retweeted political stuff: riots in India, the misadventures of Conservative MPs and journalists and aristocrats in Britain, the global Right and their 'supremacist delusions'. But on her Instagram page were pictures of restaurants and cafés and fancy resorts and books propped up on her flawless lap on beaches. The latest was a spread of fresh fruits and cheese and wine with a comment on how awful it was to be away from family in Surrey. I checked her Twitter and there was a new post, a link about a white woman who called the cops on a group of black kids playing in a public space, shared about the same time as her last Instagram post. I began to do a side by side comparison of her posts on both platforms and saw that Twitter was for her politics and Instagram was a place for documenting what she described, in one throwback picture of her trip to St Helena, as 'the embrace and performance of radical joy'. The corresponding tweet to the St Helena photo was a thread on her grandparents' journey as 'Afro-Asians of Gujarati' origins from post-colonial Kenya to England 'in the late 60s' and how they lost everything and started from scratch, raising her parents who became accomplished doctors. I saw that Kabumba had replied with stories about Indians who were driven out of Uganda. He and Sara went back and forth drawing lines of similarities between 'that history' and the 'present moment' and what 'we can learn from the past'.

I was about to return to my Dos Passos when Perky's second text came in – 'I see you and I know' – and I could see her typing a follow-up text.

I waited but nothing came through.

I looked up to make sure there wasn't a camera in my room. Maybe it was the whisky, or just my imagination, but I felt a sudden strong conviction that the whole programme was a reality show of some sort, with secret cameras monitoring our every move. The more I imagined it the more real it became, our private lives broadcast to a secret audience somewhere, perhaps a cluster of audiences scattered around the world.

I laughed at this thought and tried to dismiss it as the combined blow of weed and whisky. My homeless buddy had said something about 'minor side effects' and how the 'ingredients' might 'uplift you'.

I continued to look around for cameras, and slowly the reality of spying apparatuses somewhere in my room became so strong I started moving things around, and after a while I saw myself in the hallway looking up and down and sideways for cameras or anything that could confirm my suspicion, tiptoeing as I made my slow progress.

I heard laughter in Sara's room. I lingered. She was speaking a language I didn't understand. I put my ear against her door. More laughter. Voices. She was skyping or zooming, switching between languages, English and something else. It was almost midnight in Boston. She said something about moving her 'camera' and asked if the other person could 'see better'. The possibility of discovering something new about Sara somehow cancelled my hunt for spy cameras. It became so strong I ignored the possibility of someone coming out to see me standing there in my faded pink boxers and white singlet. I held my breath and leaned in closer but I was having a hard time standing still and my vision was beginning to blur. I shuffled a little and I sensed the sudden silence coming from her room. I pulled back from the door, missed my balance and bumped against the wall behind me. I heard Sara's voice ringing out from within, 'Who's there?' I made a sharp turn, scurrying down the hallway. Just as I was about to pass Kabumba's room he emerged forcefully, having heard Sara's voice, wielding his Maasai stick and ready to attack. We collided so hard I tumbled and landed on my back and he fell to one side. He scrambled up and I lay where I was, facing up. Claudia González and Deepak had emerged from their respective rooms, looking at the scene, while Sara and Kabumba stood close to me. The shirtless Kabumba, wearing *kente* pyjama bottoms, broke the silence with a statement that I thought was unnecessary and a little dramatic. 'You are drunk.' He repeated it and I offered him a wide grin before crawling on all fours back to my room.

The next day I saw Perky's follow-up text. The one from the previous night was meant for someone else. I also received two emails from her, one from her official address and the other from her Gmail account. The former was to inform me of a meeting with the programme committee in relation to the hallway 'incident'; the latter provided notes on those who sent the complaint – Sara and Kabumba – and she wondered if I was considering moving out of Comstock Place. She knew a friend in town with a room to spare. I ignored the emails.

That afternoon I went to the mail room in the Humanities Building, not because I was expecting a mail or any package. It was just a matter of habit, a product of working at the post office back home.

My pigeonhole was empty but I stood and peered in as though something would appear. As I was leaving, I heard someone come in from the door to my left. I turned and saw that it was Kabumba. He was busy prodding his pigeonhole with his African stick, holding and sucking on a popsicle with his other hand. I was about to leave when he called out my name without looking in my direction. I froze and rigidly turned and waved. He pointed his stick at me and asked me to wait. He advanced and I thought I might defuse the tension with an apology for 'what happened last night'. I began to speak and he waved his popsicle. 'Nah, don't worry about it.' He branched out into a different subject, wondering why, 'just out of curiosity', I avoided the 'other Africans' on campus. He had invited me to a number of events but I had ignored them all. We as 'Africans should always stick together'. I nodded and wanted to correct him and say, 'It's *you* that I've been avoiding', but I didn't and hoped he would summarise his speech. He carried on. He paused to suck on his popsicle. I could sense another line of advice or accusation brewing inside him. I made to go, but he asked, 'So how's the writing?' and laughed out loud in response to his own question. I don't know what came over me but it was quick and decisive. I charged and plucked the popsicle from his mouth and snatched his stick. He leaped back in horror and I staggered, disoriented by my own act of violence. I threw the stick in front of him, and in a moment of rare confidence I declared that I wasn't interested in his Africa, wasn't interested in Sara's 'post-colonial world', wasn't interested in any world, and 'I no longer care about this fucking programme.'

As I turned to leave, I saw the dean and Kathryn and Perky and a group of undergraduates standing by the stairs leading to the classrooms on the second floor.

I lowered my head and walked away as fast as I could.

I spent the whole day in my room, and spent the rest of the week avoiding my emails, unable to go outside, until a call from Iris broke my mood with the promise of escape.

She was back in the US and was 'reaching out' to invite me to Maine to 'catch up' and see 'that part of the country'. A friend of hers from college grew up on Moose Island on the coast of Maine and had recently decided to move back there after years working as an 'international development expert in DC and Rwanda'. Iris herself thought it would be nice to have her own 'place' to return to whenever she was 'in the country'. So she had bought her own 'place up there' in the same town, and since she was 'in the country' she thought it 'would be great' to host me 'a second time' in a 'different world'.

And so I hauled my arse out of Boston and out of my despair and saw myself in a place so far from everything else in the US that I thought I was either in Canada or in a territory that had long severed ties with the rest of the country, with towns and settlements whose names, when I looked up the state itself, transported me to places outside the United States: Poland, Cambridge, China, Mexico, Naples, Dresden, Paris, Belfast, Bath, Carthage, Moscow, Bristol, Newcastle, Wales, Belgrade, York. And these were interspersed with native American names for towns and rivers and lakes and counties: Piscataquis, Androscoggin, Kennebec, Aroostook, Narraguagus, Penobscot, Sagadahoc, Piscataqua.

Throughout the train ride from Boston to Brunswick I kept looking at the map and out the window and googling towns and places in Maine, reading blogs and articles, and I began to form the impression that there was something raw and old and experienced and tired but also knowing and freeing about the place. I shared this with Iris on the car ride from Brunswick to Moose Island and she laughed and said I sounded like everyone else who saw Maine as 'some fabled location where time had stopped'. I mentioned a piece I'd read on the train, by one 'progressive writer and third generation Mainer' and '420 advocate' who lamented 'a certain tendency' by some writers and critics to see Maine as a backwater occupied by 'simpleminded country folks' and rough-looking lobster men and fishermen, a place without 'colour or warmth'. He took aim at Elizabeth Hardwick's 'In Maine', published many years ago in the *New York Review of Books*, from which he quoted generously and which, to my surprise, he compared to 'how some see Africa as a land of darkness'. 'Hardwick's Maine,' he wrote, 'is a primitive landscape where "every stone is a skull and you live close to your own death. Where, you ask yourself, where indeed will I be buried?" Her Mainers are paranoid: "always predicting hordes of one kind or another, tourists, summer house buyers, marinas, dense developments from the icy tip to the barely warm south". The locals are always "puttering, dreaming, working".' He dragged in another writer whose more recent piece described his journey from southern Maine to the Canadian border as 'a journey through the wastelands of a type of America that most Americans won't recognise'.

The same writer, as the '420 advocate' pointed out, had himself written a scathing review of a book of 'American impressions' by a French writer whose account 'lacked a true and faithful and nuanced understanding of the complexities of the United States', and whose position was a relic of 'your typical European views of America as a land of religious "cranks" and bigots, individualistic "nutjobs" and political busybodies, gun-slinging nationalists and conspiracy theorists'.

I felt the Mainer's pain reading his piece, and I understood him well. But it was also entertaining, imagining him writhing in his powerlessness, unable to undo the stereotypes about his beloved state, unable to stop what he had described as that 'look you see and know in the eyes of some seasonal residents and tourists who see everything and everyone around here as some prop and background for their summer'.

I wanted to share with Iris how much his piece reminded me of Chinua Achebe's response to Conrad's *Heart of Darkness*, which the Mainer's piece had also referenced in a way that would make sense to anyone who had read Conrad's novella before encountering Achebe's piece.

We drove past the historic district of a town along Route 1, where stately houses from the eighteenth and nineteenth centuries lined its quiet streets.

Iris said it used to be a port town, and the massive houses, which now seemed alien in comparison to all I had seen along the way, were built by shipbuilders and sea captains from a time when the town prospered from the thriving 'seafaring business'. Ships from here, I imagined, must have made their way to Port Jumbo and other ports on the Atlantic coast, carrying produce and human cargo.

I did look up the town days later and confirmed that some of its prominent residents and others along the coast had participated in the slave trade as owners or captains of slave vessels, a revelation that retroactively justified how I thought of myself as Conrad on a mission up the coast.

Unlike Conrad in the Congo, my destination wasn't a hideous spot in a mysterious wilderness; Iris's house was a renovated historic home built in the early nineteenth century, and it sat on a highland overlooking the Narrow Black River estuary, with a generous view of the ocean in the distance.

And her friends who 'came over' later that night were neither Kurtz, the notorious ivory trader in Conrad's *Heart of Darkness*, nor the silent 'savages' in the same novella. They were sophisticated professionals who looked nothing like 'puttering' bumpkins and lumberjacks and hardened leftovers from the seafaring past. They had well-defined careers that upset my sense of worth. There was an osteopath slash yoga instructor who counterbalanced her background in 'Western practices' with months of training with a 'master' in some Indian village; the other was an investment banker slash part-time instructor at a local university; there was a founder of an addiction treatment facility 'near Bangor'; and then the friend who'd moved up to Maine before Iris.

The group reminded me of the expats that I met at Iris's place back home in Nigeria. Different worlds but a similar vibe: a gathering of the polite for the polite.

On one side, the osteopath and the addiction expert were listening to the investment banker talking about the rise of 'microbreweries' and giving a mini lecture on the 'craft beers' he'd brought up for us, especially the one from a small company 'down in Portland' that his team had invested in. And on the other side, Iris and her friend Carol were arranging light refreshments for the evening.

Carol's house, which I saw earlier, was a walking distance from Iris's. At one point that evening I went outside and saw the Narrow Black River slithering towards the Atlantic and I knew, as Iris had shared, that the closest spot to Africa from the United States was located just an hour north of where I was standing. I tried to imagine what it would be like living out there in that town further north. My imagination failed me, just as it failed when I tried to picture the evening ahead with Iris and her friends. I was still scarred by my experience at the Kirkpatricks. It didn't help that on the drive up from Brunswick Iris had casually said something about Boston and the 'long email she got from her mother', and how she, Iris, was 'sincerely sorry that' I had to 'go through all that'. She had said it in a rather flat and unaffected way so I wasn't sure if she was on my side or her mother's. I got the impression that her mother had reported the dinner incident as a case of cultural difference that resulted in me getting 'offended', which then caused her so much pain that she had reached out to Iris to seek guidance on how 'to make amends'. Iris did not share what she advised her mother, and this gap in her remark caused me much anxiety. I wanted to know. I also wished she had waited until the end of my trip to Maine to bring it up but I guessed it was only natural to raise the issue and clear the air beforehand. But my anxiety was unfounded: the guests left earlier than expected, and it was just Iris, Carol and myself.

After months 'outside the US' working on reports and training and attending conferences and consulting for African governments and 'private sector' partners, both ladies were too 'exhausted by it all' to start talking about Africa, and were not interested in their immediate American environment because it was 'too disconnected from the real world'.

Carol said she was going to her mother's to pick up some weed for anxiety and asked if I wanted to come with. I was lounging on Iris's 'Bauhaus-inspired divan' and consuming her California Cabernet and pretending to listen to what was being said when Carol's question stirred me up. It wasn't the casual mention of marijuana that roused me but the possibility of seeing more of the area.

The drive turned out to be uneventful, about twenty minutes through back country roads with nothing remarkable: abandoned sheds, an open field with cows grazing, unpaved side roads retreating into mysterious areas.

Carol's mother's house, when we pulled up, was a far cry from her daughter's. It looked like an abandoned property that was sinking into its foundation. Back in Nigeria, this would be a stain on Carol's accomplishments and apparent financial success.

Unlike Iris's, Carol's childhood was marked by lack and violence: a father who drank himself to death, relatives with drug problems, a mother who dropped out of high school to be with Carol's father.

Carol herself was born and raised in that same house, as she later shared, and had fled west to Stanford for college, returning east to DC for graduate school, and chose a career in international development communications because she wanted to see the world and be as far away as possible.

When we entered her mother's house that day and I saw the clutter of clothes and items of all sorts piled up on the couch and floor and every surface, I pictured the world Carol had extracted herself from.

We waited a few minutes for Carol's mother to finish her phone call. She was leaving a long voicemail for her senator about a 'racist attack' on a group of Somali immigrants in a town further inland in the south-west corner of Maine.

When I was later introduced she hugged me and apologised profusely for how messy the place was, and apologised even more for how immigrants were being treated in her country. She launched into a short speech on how the United States should remain a land of 'hope and opportunity' for all and how heart-breaking it was to see the hostility 'coming from people who should know better'. Carol asked, 'Do they really know better?' I said it was all the same everywhere, the human condition, and Lori, Carol's mother, drew back a little as if to make sense of what I was saying, perhaps surprised that I did not attach much importance to what she had told us.

The TV in her living room was on CNN and I could hear another TV in one of the rooms with a true crime programme running. Lori and Carol squeezed through stacked boxes and books, and disappeared into the back room. Iris, who had been there before, led me to the wall where photographs of Lori with figures from 'her hippie era' hung: one with John Lennon 'somewhere in New York', another with a group of 'Americans in Tangier', and one in Mexico where she was the only woman in what looked like a campsite in a desert. Iris showed me a bookcase in one corner, and said there were signed first editions of books by 'the likes of Noam Chomsky'. I began to make my way to the bookcase, slowed down by the straight line of old charcoal clothes irons. I stopped when I heard Lori's voice, and I turned to see Carol looking gloomy and in a hurry to leave.

It was on the car ride back to her place that Carol shared that Lori had told her about the tragic drug overdose of two friends Carol knew growing up, how one of the bodies wasn't found for days because he had died in the basement of his house.

Apparently it wasn't uncommon, the drug epidemic ravaging that region, cutting down the young like dead trees. I'd read something about it a while ago, a piece by an activist in New York raising awareness but also calling out the double standards on how the drug epidemic among white Americans was reported and handled, with it being attributed to social and economic and systemic issues, not a pathology linked to whiteness, and certainly not an issue that required 'the leaders of the white community' to stand up and act on behalf of some 'mythical white community', just a social problem that required the right attention. Carol had said something along those lines, the need for 'a comprehensive solution'.

Iris, perhaps drained by the topic, swerved the conversation to Lori's apology about the US; she herself apologised for Lori's generalisation, and said something about 'a certain generation of white women' in a context that I didn't get. She turned to look at me in the back seat. In response, to move the conversation further away, I said I wasn't bothered at all, that I was instead thinking about what Carol had said earlier on the way to her mother's, something about the business of cannabis, how much money it was generating in states where it was legal.

To lighten the mood, I said the world might just be a better place if more countries legalised marijuana, especially poor countries in Africa and South America where the boost in national income could have positive impact, not to forget the overall boost to peace and calm, and how many wars would end if the warring parties were prescribed the right strain of anxiety-combating slash eliminating cannabis to alter their consciousness from unnecessary anger and hostility. Encouraged by their laughter, I invited them to imagine a US foreign policy driven by the 'chill-out potential' of a special strain of cannabis.

I may have gone too far when I shared an imaginary strategy of planting 'a whole army' of secret agents to systematically introduce pro-marijuana laws to countries, drumming up a market for that strain of US-grown cannabis.

There was silence, followed by Iris's remark about a journalist friend of hers who recently published an investigative piece on the abuse of prescription drugs containing codeine in northern Nigeria. Carol said she had read the piece and knew of similar cases in Liberia.

And once again the conversation shifted back to me and my world and the woes of my continent. They knew more about Africa than I did. They knew its policies and how much money flowed in from the United States and what happened to that money. They had more ammunition to win the little Cold War that I had unwittingly started.

■

That night, after the awkward battle, we drank heavily and avoided any subject that remotely referenced the events of the day. The vow of silence meant that I couldn't say what I was thinking about the board game we were playing as we drank, the one where you placed train tracks on a map of the United States, scoring points as the tracks grew and expanded across the continent, gaining additional points if you possessed the longest track. It was a history of the United States in one board, its expansions and possessions, its domination and transformation of spaces, and I could see both coasts shrunk into a single, continuous line of movement, a circulation of violence and entanglement and progress and achievement.

I tried to imagine the game from the perspective of a Native American, tried to imagine the embedded violence of receiving rewards for laying train tracks across lands and territories and histories, and I wondered if Iris and Carol had thought of it that way.

I came last twice and found myself wanting to win at least once. I asked for tips. I strategised. I laid tracks in places that prevented my opponents from making progress or gaining access to their intended routes. I could feel the combined thrust of fear and confidence as I marched across the land, aiming for the longest track, a route that zigzagged from Charleston to San Francisco; and I felt something weird when Carol, chuckling, laid tracks between Phoenix and Los Angeles, cutting me off, and I lost again, stranded in El Paso, at the US–Mexico border. Her chuckle grew into a full laugh, as Iris tallied up the points, and I sat there irritated but going along with it, suppressing the urge to throw in a malicious comment about the stories that often came out of that border. But it was over in no time, the drinks flowed and my savage impulses were calmed by the civilised taste of wine. And I was glad I held my tongue, because what followed afterwards, later into the night, would not have happened if I'd soiled the mood with a petty reference to the border.

It was on the train back to Boston the next day, when I was piecing together how we went from that game to talking about how we might never see each other again because Iris was sure she wouldn't return to Nigeria to huddling together on Iris's enormous couch like teenagers at a party, that it occurred to me that what happened was a remarkable first for me: the warmth of three bodies in the same bed, an experience I'd only enjoyed in numerous fantasies. And its ordinariness, how natural it was – though the drinks helped – shifted the way I saw the world, and brought me closer to my own sexuality. Besides, it was my second sexual encounter in America. More sex in one season than in my whole adult life put together.

12

S OON after I returned from Maine, Perky sent round a reminder about an upcoming event in New York, organised by the programme, in partnership with Sinclair Davis Literary, a boutique agency that specialises in 'new voices in world literature'. I *did* go to New York but managed to avoid the whole event. I did my own thing instead. Their plan was to go up and engage in a series of literary orgies: meetings with agents, 'pitching' (how I hate that word) our books and book ideas to publishers, 'cocktails' (another word I loathe) with publishers, informal dinners with some established 'world writers of the American experience'. And the highlight would be a one-to-one with the British-born and US-raised Sinclair Davis, the so-called bad boy of the publishing world, who could, as everyone said, transform a rickshaw wallah in Delhi into a *New York Times* bestselling memoirist. It was he, that literary buccaneer, who handpicked and gave the world Bobby Pickerel, author of the three-volume *Memoirs of a Caribbean Sailor in New York*, which subsequently made Pickerel the prince and spokesperson of contemporary world literature. It was also Davis who defended Pickerel when the Irish poet Sally O'Connor accused him of slapping her arse at a writers' retreat in Havana.

We were to fly to New York together and stay at some house in Brooklyn, a block from where the great Freddie Jones lived and wrote his world-famous comic novels of life in Depression-era New York. We would have access to coffee and breakfast at Ricky's Rebellion Shack, where you were sure to spot a poet or novelist or librettist drowning in coffee and reeking of last night's whisky.

It was a dream for the Kabumbas of this world, a chance to simultaneously kiss the arses and suckle the enormous tits of the great huntresses of talent while calling them out at the same time. I pictured Kabumba in his Maasai toga, sprinkling each introduction with a Swahili phrase, supporting his own remarks with a long-lost proverb, pointing his stick to an imaginary arid landscape populated by dying shrubs and children squeezing milk from the dry udders of malnourished cows. I had no doubts about him being the centre of attention.

And he had work to show, his stupid *Sisters of the Lake District*. For this reason, I swore not to attend. I knew I wasn't a marketable African writer. I lacked the temperament of a socially conscious black writer. And how could I compete with Kabumba's teeth-flashing smile and thunderous laughter?

And there was something else, an embarrassing experience I had from a similar 'meet and pitch' event at a different writing programme in Boston. There, standing before a noted recruiter of 'ethnic writers making a difference', it occurred to me that I had no difference-making ideas to 'pitch', nothing to bring to the fabled 'conversation'.

I tried to pitch her my George Thompson story but I was unable to roll the whole thing into a pitchable sentence. My mouth dried. I gasped, 'I love those earrings; are they from West Africa?' No, they weren't, and she flushed and I scurried out the door.

'But you *must* come with us to New York,' said Perky, 'it's a core part of your fellowship. Or you risk becoming what everyone already thinks of you.'

'What, a total arsehole? If they already think that of me, it's probably best to keep it that way by skipping your great literary orgy.'

How, then, to escape? A practical question. Announce that an untreated case of malaria had flared up and I must seek immediate help?

I cooked up a plan: to go by bus, which I said I'd pay for with my own money, and to leave two days early to explore the city before the 'meet and pitch'. I added a last excuse for taking the bus: I wanted to see the East Coast as clearly as I could. But I knew I would not show up at all for the event, and was already planning a last-minute excuse – a delayed train in New York, maybe a sudden case of diarrhoea.

I went on Airbnb and booked a place in Washington Heights, hosted by one Cattie. It promised wi-fi and free coffee, and it was terribly cheap compared to everything else I saw.

I messaged Cattie: '... in New York for market survey for a new coffee-growing social venture in southern Nigeria...'

I wasn't required to share the purpose of my trip, but I had a suspicion that Cattie wasn't the kind who'd leave you alone.

That broad smile. That lavish 'mi casa es su casa' description on her page. Better to feed her something false and take it from there.

The day came. I left on the 11 a.m. Bolt Bus from South Station. The passengers, some silent and some already falling asleep, would disappoint any foreigner who imagined travelling Americans to be talkative and restless.

I fell asleep in no time, and missed everything between Boston and New Haven.

In New York, we were spat out on the curb, between Eleventh Avenue and West 36th Street. I looked around at all the tall buildings and began to find my way to Penn Station.

After several useless turns and irritated by the misleading routes my phone was showing, I asked a black man who assumed I spoke Spanish. He shared instructions in that language. I politely nodded and bounded on in the wrong direction.

Just after a Mexican grill, the rollers on my suitcase broke. It began to make a squeaky sound on the sidewalk. A police officer standing nearby asked, perhaps out of sheer irritation, 'You OK, buddy?'

'I'm fine,' I replied and carried on.

I took a turn and when I raised my eyes I saw Penn Station ahead.

I knew my destination. Cattie had sent me instructions that began at Penn Station and ended at her doorstep.

I bought my tickets, took the A train to Station Street and walked to the address Cattie had given.

I pushed the button and the elevator descended, looking like an enormous coffin.

I entered and was whisked up to another realm. The fifth floor.

Mandy, who Cattie had already mentioned in her messages, welcomed me at the door. She, Cattie and a third roommate shared the apartment. In due course I'd find out they were all recent graduates of Harrison University, just north of the city, where they'd studied theatre arts, and were presently temping around New York.

My room was next to the bathroom – a narrow, rectangular room that had barely enough space for the bed. The window opened to a view of another apartment building standing squarely across the street like a bully.

When Cattie came back from her temp job, she recommended a few 'nice Dominican restaurants around' where I could get something authentic. She made sure to share how she and her friends bought local to keep the money circulating in the neighbourhood. Something about fighting or offsetting the impact of gentrification that I didn't understand.

I ignored her recommendation, went online and ordered myself a General Tso's Chicken from a place that called itself The Red Flower on Broadway. General Tso came with broccoli and boiled white rice. It was tasty. I saved the leftovers.

Hours later, around 10 p.m., I had an urge to enter the city and walk around, but I killed that idea. I stood at the window facing the other building, looked left and saw Broadway, the steady stream of traffic and bodies. I tried to work up an appetite for rambling, to enter the so-called charm and beauty of the city at night, but it didn't work.

I told myself it was all pointless anyway. My head was already full of stories and images of the city by those who'd walked and written about it. No need to go out and walk or think of writing about it. How could one possibly write about New York without sounding like everyone else? There was absolutely nothing new about the city. Each new book, claiming a new approach, ended up sounding like the last. There were books that mourned the death of old New York, books that described the present New York, and books about books on New York. An endless cycle. And every now and then some bored chap with a PhD in English or art history or the like would do a book on this or that artist or writer or dancer who lived in the Village and rubbed shoulders with Andy Warhol, et cetera, et cetera. And the book would spend its first chapter justifying how it wasn't like any other book about New York. And from time to time, some literary journalist would drum up a book about a nearly forgotten New York socialite, like the one about Beatrice Dover and her bohemian circle in the fifties.

Anyone with a television and a grade-school education could picture New York from a million miles away. I had my stock mental pictures of fictional protagonists who I imagined everywhere in New York: a lone guy, preferably single after a bad divorce (or single because he's an arsehole pretending to be single by choice); a new immigrant fleeing the horrors of war in Europe or the Middle East or Africa; some chap from the South or Midwest newly arrived to cut his teeth as a writer; a cultural critic 'curating' notes for a book on art and alienation.

All you needed to do was to picture and follow these creatures as they went from one busy street to another, boring you to death with their extended interior monologues, their narcissistic first-person indulgences.

And if *you* were the protagonist, doing the walking yourself, you would find yourself entering some godforsaken record store in Harlem where a battered vinyl would remind you of a certain golden decade in the history of jazz.

And if you were lucky enough to walk past a certain café near Columbia University, on a given summer day, you'd spot Whitman and Ashbery in the flesh, sharing a joint and chatting in quatrains.

It's all been done, I told myself. And I was feeling content. Though not for long, as I suddenly realised I really was in New York without a solid plan. People go to New York to *do* something or *be* something. To see the Statue of Liberty or go to the Whitney. To cross Brooklyn Bridge on foot or see where the Twin Towers once stood. To drink where Norman Mailer drank. To see Poe's cottage in the Bronx. I had no plans and wasn't interested in doing what I could easily read or look up somewhere. Going to the William Blake event was out of the question. Picturing Kabumba there and imagining myself among those idea-pitching upbeat phoneys caused me much anxiety.

I tucked myself into the small bed, which was rather too short to contain my whole length. My feet stuck out. I connected my phone to Cattie's wi-fi, plugged in my red headphones and logged on to my favourite porn site.

I searched for my favourite performance, which always guaranteed a relaxing, anxiety-conquering climax. I checked the number of views at the bottom of the video, as I always did, and each increase was a sign that I wasn't alone in my obsession. A whopping four million. I smiled and clicked on the play icon. They were on the same large bed: Tory Tumble, Joan Vicar and Lucy Juggernaut. The last two, despite their names, spoke and moaned in some Slavic accent, while Tory Tumble, built like a fire truck, moaned in some version of Australian English.

I spared myself the preamble and skipped ahead to where the action was reminiscent of gladiators locked together, naked bodies slipping off one another.

And just as my excitement climbed, I overheard voices at the door. Expressions of disgust and hilarity. 'What the fuck?' from one voice. And loud laughter from another.

Alarmed, I took the headphones out of my ears, and to my greatest horror, the *ohs* and *ahs* of Tory, Joan and Lucy were still audible. The headphones hadn't gone all the way in.

I frantically tried to conceal the phone under my blanket, to smother the voices at once, my hands trembling. Before I knew it, the phone slipped and fell to the floor. And since I had accidentally trapped one end of the headphone under the blanket, it detached itself from the phone, as if to say, 'I have no hand in your nasty business,' thus amplifying the whole thing at the precise moment Joan Vicar (I knew this from memory) screamed in performed pleasure, 'Ooooh yeaaahhh, fuck that…' and in one last act squealed, 'YES, YES, YES,' which of course, as I also knew from memory, was the part where Tumble pulled out of Vicar and came on Lucy Juggernaut's tits, accompanied by his energetic truck-like groan.

Outside my door: 'Sooo fucking disgusting' from one voice, and another bolt of laughter from the second.

I scrambled off the bed, lost my balance and crash-landed on my suitcase.

Pouncing on the phone, I turned it off.

I heard Cattie's voice, 'It's OK, Frank, we've all been there.'

She was clearly the one who thought it was funny. Or did she?

'By the way,' she continued, 'we're watching the Kardashians and there's an open bottle of red.'

'The Kardashians?' I was hugging my suitcase at this point, blinking uncontrollably as if to wish away the whole fiasco. 'The Kardashians?' I repeated to myself. I had heard of the show but never seen it. And I surely didn't want to. But Cattie had me. I knew she knew I was trapped. I had to pay for my nasty act by saying yes to her offer. And by saying yes, I would have to face everyone, to offer myself up and be humiliated.

'We're cool,' Mandy said when I sank into the sofa across from the television.

Mandy was the one who'd expressed disgust at first. Skinny. Piercings on her lower lip, tongue, around her right ear. A set of beads around her left ankle. She gave me a comprehensive look, and I had the impression she'd seen into my soul and found me miserable but somewhat cute, which, perhaps, explained why she grinned after saying, 'We're cool,' before returning to fiddling with her phone.

The third roommate wasn't home. She'd gone to see her boyfriend in Brooklyn, a lecturer at some college.

One bottle became two, then three. More episodes of the Kardashians, which we hardly watched but left on as some accessory for the night.

Cattie had stopped knitting whatever it was she was knitting for her cousin. She was now leading the conversation, moving from one subject to another, pausing only to ask what we thought, running off before those thoughts barely saw the light. Now we were talking about rent in New York, a subject that I knew nothing about. But I hazarded a generic line, 'How sad for those who see their beloved neighbourhoods going to the highest bidder.'

She started talking about the wine shop around the corner, where the storekeeper had a metal barricade to stop customers from stepping in, and where you had to point through bars to indicate the bottle you wanted.

Mandy was gone a few minutes and came back with a pink bong. I'd never seen a bong in real life. They showed me the ropes. I learned fast.

Cattie asked a string of questions about my 'coffee business', about Nigeria, about my life as a social entrepreneur.

I shared what I had planned to share: 'So, there's this rich guy whose dad made his money in oil, and he wanted to do something different from what his father did, so he came to me… I mean, I've known the guy for ten years, we were in school together, and he knew I had a degree in agro-sustainability and microbusiness growth, and knew I'd spent a year working for a social venture in Ghana. So, I advised him to buy a hundred acres outside Port Jumbo, and we planted coffee, interspersed with legumes below and trees above. The coffee will be ready in a year, and that's why I'm in New York, to meet a select number of buyers, just as I'm planning to do in San Francisco, in London, Paris, Berlin and a few other cities.'

Mandy handed me the bong.

Inspired by my robust account, Mandy jumped and said, 'I just had an idea, and I'd like to know what you guys think.'

She wanted to start an exclusive mafia tour of the city, through all the places and streets where mafia killings had happened, like those Jack the Ripper tours in London.

A great idea, Cattie and I echoed deliriously, and then reeled off a few suggestions. Why not break it down into factions from which tourists could pick: Italian Mafia Tour, Irish Mob Tour, Jewish Mafia Tour, Corrupt Cops of the 75th Precinct Tour. Those were Cattie's idea. Mine: have costumes ready for willing tourists and plant re-enactors at every stop: a policeman loading arrested mobsters into a van, mutilated bodies lying on the sidewalk, prostitutes dashing out of a motel, chased by cops.

Mandy took notes on her phone, ostensibly serious about our suggestions, and then she invited us to join her on the couch for a group selfie for her Instagram page. She took multiple shots and said something about having fun with 'friends'. She showed me her Instagram page, which said at the top that she was a 'Social Influencer, Lover of Life, Nomad, Stylist and Modern Witch'.

Cattie threw the window open.

The city wafted in, thick with fumes and dust.

For no reason, other than, well, the contents of the bong and the wine itself, Mandy went to the window and howled into the night, 'Ahoooo.'

We laughed out of rhythm. It was the weekend after all. And I felt triumphant over Kabumba, who I imagined wasn't having as much fun wherever he was.

In a moment of total out-of-control-ness, fuelled by sheer elation at my luck – I mean, I was partying for free with two free-spirited ladies – I said, 'I fucking love America,' and like Mandy I went and brayed into the night, 'I fucking love the United Fucking States of Americaaaaah,' slurring every single word. Both girls rewarded me with their disconcerted, wine-fuelled laughter, and a lone voice rang out from the building across: 'Shut the fuck up, ahhhsole.'

I caught myself wondering what was happening to me, my sudden avowed love for America. The worrying part was that I couldn't tell if Cattie and Mandy were really that carefree or just enjoying a rather goofy night with a miserable creature like me. I also wondered if they were all they said they were, or if they'd also made up stories just to keep the night as fantastic as it was, to be as unrealistic as we all wanted to be.

The response to my window howl – 'Shut the fuck up, ahhh-sole' – shook me a bit. The voice had a ring of sincerity to it, and in a quick second I imagined its owner as some chap in a love-hate relationship with America, unsure why the country I was professing my alcohol-inspired love for wasn't loving him back. This thought killed my buzz.

I took my leave, holding the walls of the corridor to my room, taking a detour to the kitchen where I exhumed and consumed what was left of General Tso's Chicken before trudging back to retire for the night.

I woke up early the next morning without a hangover. Something to do with the Chinese food, I guessed. I went to the window and fixed my eyes on the window across the street, waiting to see if the voice that responded last night would appear and declare itself. I looked down and saw a line of dumpsters. There was a guy dumping a plastic bag in one of them, lingering over it as though waiting for some miracle to happen. Broadway was still where I had left it last night, visible to my left, filled with cars and pedestrians.

To avoid the awkwardness of spending daytime with Cattie and her roommates, I set out early like people with a purpose do. But I had no purpose. No destination.

Perky had sent me a text earlier. 'Let me know how you're doing.'

I replied as the elevator descended, 'Doing just fine.'

I turned right on Broadway, walked for a few blocks, passed Boricua College and saw the Hispanic Society building, a place I 'knew' from a novel I read many years ago. I said to myself, 'Here's something to do.' But the Hispanic Society was closed for renovation.

I went right on West 155th, towards the river, passed the American Numismatic Society and stopped when I saw the American Academy of Art and Letters.

I asked an elderly woman walking out of the building to take a photo of me by the plaque at the entrance. She took my phone. I saw her name tag, Julia Ward Howe, a name that was vaguely familiar, that I'd either read or heard about, and I almost asked if she was a poet.

Walking on, I spotted a man on Riverside Drive. He looked about my age, in a red shirt that was missing a sleeve, torn from neck to back. He was screaming and jumping near the entrance to Trinity Cemetery. I knew Ralph Ellison was somewhere in that cemetery, and I wanted to go in. But the screaming man was approaching me. I quickened my pace and soon lost him. I crossed the road, took a step down, closer now to the river.

Feeling like a tourist, I asked a man in running shoes and jogging pants if that was New Jersey on the other side of the river.

'You mean the Hudson River?' he asked. 'Yes, it's New Jersey.'

'Wow,' I said, and he drew back and hurried off.

I knew it was New Jersey. But I just felt compelled to ask someone.

I walked a few paces and took the steps down on 148th Street, towards Riverside Gardens, where I sat for about an hour, listening to the river, watching boats sailing back and forth, and the birds perching on the wire fence a few steps ahead.

Hours later, after many aimless turns and stops, I found myself in Harlem. I recall how it felt like I was back in Port Jumbo, on a busy street with children and their parents flowing back and forth at ease.

I entered a café and was surprised to see that every single customer was white and young, on their iPhones and MacBooks. It was as if they'd been herded into that small space, away from the predominantly black population outside.

Interestingly, the baristas were black, and it appeared they were so used to a certain species of customers that my presence unsettled them a little. I wasn't in the mood to wait around to understand or endure that layer of cultural politics. I turned and headed across the street to a pub.

Inside, couples and friends were everywhere. New Yorkers unwinding.

After my third pint, I began to ask the bartender a series of questions. To the question, 'Are you from Puerto Rico?' (everyone seemed to be from Puerto Rico or the Dominican Republic), he said he was half-black and half-Irish, and I defensively said I was half-Nigerian and half-Sierra Leonean, to which he nodded as if I was speaking Latin.

I said, 'Well, guess I'm just one hundred per cent black, eh?'

He raised an eyebrow, and I shut my mouth for a minute or two before asking, 'So, were you born here in Hahlahm?'

Yes, he was, and he talked about the changes 'around here', a topic I knew would come up in no time, since I figured it was a favourite subject 'around here'.

Seeing how he kept casting an evil stare at a customer sitting on a stool to my far left, I dared to ask, 'Who's that guy, a famous person?'

'Famous?' the bartender sneered. 'Just a regular douchebag.'

It turned out the douchebag was from Romania, new to New York, and the bartender had recently overheard him talking to someone on his phone, saying he was at least white in America and that counted for something, unlike in London where he used to live, where he was just another guy from Eastern Europe.

I was about to ask the bartender another question when a group flowed in through the door, forming a semicircle behind and around me, right there at the bar. One of them, a tall black lady with long eyelashes, was talking rapidly about a 'newly woke white bitch', who wouldn't stop tweeting about the suffering of 'black and brown people' and wouldn't stop talking about it everywhere at every opportunity, to the distress of her black and brown friends, and the group agreed that yes, the white bitch was annoying.

Two curious figures walked in, cutting through the group to plant themselves next to me at the bar. A skinny Fulani-looking man wearing a djellaba, with prayer beads wrapped around his wrist; and a stout, bearded, boyish-looking man adjusting his satin yarmulke. At first it seemed I was the only one surprised to see two religious men ordering shots at the bar. But after their second shot, when they began to talk animatedly in Arabic, the raucous group paused to consider them. Both men seemed upset about something and didn't take note of the curious stares their presence invited. After a third shot they went straight through the group and disappeared. I took that as my cue to leave.

I paused in the middle of the room to reply Perky's text asking where I was.

'I'm in Harlem,' I wrote, 'in pimp.'

'What?' she replied immediately.

I saw the disaster autocorrect had wreaked.

'Oh, no,' I explained, 'fucking auto...' and I pushed send before completing the text.

Her reply: 'Wtf, Frank?'

At this point I was holding my phone tight, opening my eyes as wide as possible, trying to type out each letter with precision.

'In Harlem, in a bar.' To clear the air, I added, 'Sorry, fucking automatic...' When I saw that I'd mistyped 'autocorrect', I groaned and trudged out the door.

Back at Cattie's, nobody was home. I ordered pizza online and spent the night reading comments on a viral *Guardian* article about the death of the novel.

The next morning, on the day of the event, I went to explore the area around the venue, to see if I could find a spot from which to spy on Kabumba and the rest as they cocktailed and pitched. I found my ideal spot across the street, at a café on the ground floor of an apartment building. I chose an empty chair in the far right corner of the café, between the wall and a window. I could see the venue on the other side of the street, an art gallery that looked like a warehouse, with a wide door that gave a good view of the inside.

I saw Kabumba engaging an audience of three, all with paper plates bearing what looked like croissants. I tried to imagine what he was sharing with his audience. How he walked ten miles to school barefoot, and then twenty miles up a hill to the nearest stream after school? Or when a lion came to their village and snatched a child away in the dead of night?

You had to hand it to Kabumba. He was a seasoned performer and knew how to work an audience: how to slip from a sad story about his childhood to a long spiel on belonging and identity; from representations of Africa in the media to the merits and demerits of foreign aid.

I kept my eyes on him for a while, filled with loathing and admiration, trying and failing to understand how he sustained his acts and wondering what vacuum his stories filled in the hearts and minds of his listeners. Whatever he was selling had a ready market and it appeared both buyer and seller understood each other.

A bespectacled, clean-shaven man walked into the café, carrying a distressed leather satchel and looking a bit distressed himself. He sat next to me, fished out a folder, opened it, and I caught a glimpse of its contents, a manuscript with the title, 'The Weight of Language: New and Selected Essays'. I saw the name, William Vanleer, and I almost asked if he was the same Vanleer whose *Lolita*-inspired novel-in-verse, 'a vile and disturbing doorstopper' as one reviewer called it, had triggered a furore a year or so ago, leading to his eventual cancellation. I resisted the impulse. I went up and bought a bottle of water, and left through a side door.

13

MY absence from the New York event had sealed my reputation as *the* person to avoid. On their return to Boston, Sara and Kabumba had each tweeted passive attacks on my behaviour. While Kabumba pointed out 'the role some Africans play in perpetuating #globalblackdisrespect', Sara reminded the world of the need to start talking about the 'narcissism of a certain type of Black and Brown men', ending her tweet with Kabumba's hashtag. They retweeted each other's post, and their loyal followers retweeted, and I watched as the conversation took multiple turns across the world, from a thread on the 'dark legacies of Afro-Caribbean writers contributing to #globalblackdisrespect' to a rather vague post on '#globalblackdisrespect and the global black elite'. By the end of the day after Kabumba's hashtag, and reading Sara's subsequent subtweet alluding to 'a recent experience in New York', I knew it was time to leave Comstock Place.

I followed up on the email Perky had sent me the day after the hallway 'incident', where she wondered if I was considering moving out of Comstock, adding the line about her 'friend in town with a room to spare'. She called and said the room was still available, and she gave me Edna's contact information.

I emailed Edna, and she replied to express her delight at the possibility of sharing her 'space' with me, and said I could come 'see the room in person' or we could arrange a 'Zoom tour' if I was busy.

I didn't care either way since I'd made up my mind to leave. A change of scenery was all I needed. I looked up the address, 69 Sharpton Street, about fifteen miles south-east of the William Blake campus.

The next day, around noon, I packed my suitcase, threw on the same clothes I was wearing the day I arrived, and waited until the other fellows were out before booking an Uber.

The house on Sharpton Street was exactly as I pictured it, white, old by American standards, derelict. The neighbourhood itself, as described in comments on various internet forums, was 'sketchy'. I'd looked up what it meant for a neighbourhood to be 'sketchy' in the US. And the answers I got confirmed my suspicion: 'sketchy' was predominantly poor and non-white.

When my Uber pulled up, and I saw the untrimmed hedges and a black man relaxing on the hood of a car, eyeballing me, and saw two women whose ethnicity I couldn't tell sitting on their front porch chatting, I knew I'd indeed landed in a 'sketchy' neighbourhood, further confirmed by the overall state of the houses and the trail of trash I saw in the distance. This was exactly what I needed to feel more at home. It felt familiar, more authentic, and it 'resonated' with me (to borrow one of Sara's words).

Following the instructions Edna had texted, I let myself in. The front door was open, which intrigued me, considering the supposed sketchiness of the area. But I knew, coming from a 'sketchy' neighbourhood myself, that residents of 'sketchy' neighbourhoods had their own ways of doing things.

My room, one of three on the ground floor, was plain and simple. A narrow, single bed, a small desk, a closet.

Later that evening, after I'd napped and showered, I decided to go for a walk.

At the corner of Sharpton Street and Dorchester, I saw a place called The New Mexican Grill. I decided to go in. I took a menu and sat at a corner table. Nothing on the menu looked familiar: torta, quesadilla, chimichanga. The chimichanga sounded good.

While I waited to order, I tried to make sense of my surroundings. The servers and chefs (I could see them at the back) and customers were all… well, what were they? Hispanics, Latinos? My world and education did not prepare me to make the distinction, or to even try, the same way it didn't prepare me to care if someone was Indian or Pakistani.

When my food arrived, I took a few minutes looking at it. I was about to have Mexican for the first time in my life. I wanted to mark that moment with a brief pause.

The waitress came back and asked, 'Everything OK?'

'Everything is OK,' I said, and dug in to my first chimichanga.

There was the familiar taste of beans and rice, slightly diluted by the presence of cheese. I chewed slowly, registering the flavours, swallowing and waiting for the aftertaste before taking another bite. It was delicious.

Minutes after paying the bill and leaving, hoping to continue my walk, my stomach began to growl. Maintaining a steady pace, resisting the temptation to run, I returned to Sharpton Street and rushed to the shared bathroom.

Done with my business, I faced another crisis. The toilet had clogged. No plunger.

I panicked.

I texted Edna and waited.

No reply.

I called her and it went straight to voicemail.

I didn't leave a message. The thought of her replaying my words asking for a plunger terrified me.

I walked back to my room and saw a note on the door: *See Fridge, and Just Feel Free! Peace and Sunshine.* 'Give me a fucking plunger and keep your peace and sunshine,' I said out loud, turning to look at the stairs behind me.

A ball of irritation formed in my gut as I caught sight of the dirt-encrusted rug that ran up to Edna's flat upstairs, a far cry from the well-maintained carpets at Comstock Place. For a second the image of my bathroom at Comstock flashed before me, how pristine it was (thanks to the cleaners), its endless supply of toilet paper, not to forget how it flushed with a roaring crispness and velocity that boosted your confidence in the modern world.

Propelled by what I was feeling, I climbed the stairs, and with each step my irritation gave way to curiosity.

At her door, I was confronted by stickers protesting the Vietnam War, stickers protesting the death of Martin Luther King, Jr, stickers against the war in Iraq, against consumerism, against investment in fossil fuels, against police brutality, against Wall Street, against everything one could possibly imagine, and there was one against the invasion and colonisation of Mars. I wondered if there was a link between her politics and the absence of a plunger downstairs. This thought held me back from knocking on her door straight away. I didn't want to seem ignorant of what folks already knew about the symbolism of plungers. They do look phallic, don't they: the balls down there and handle sticking out? Is there something heteronormative about plungers that everyone knew that I didn't?

I stepped back from the door, walked two steps down the stairs, stood there and googled 'plungers + gender', scrolled about but found nothing interesting.

I walked up again and knocked twice.

A voice, unmistakably male, answered, 'Yes, yes, who's that, Frank?'

'Edna?' I asked, confused by the male voice.

'Yes,' answered the same voice, which sounded close to the door but was failing to open it, 'yes, what can I do for you, Frank?'

'Um, I think the toilet is clogged,' I said.

'You think it's clogged?'

'It *is* clogged,' I said, stepping back from the door.

'Right. It happens from time to time. But there's a plunger down there, no?'

I paused for a second, weighing the question to see if there was an undertone, a trap or something.

'Frank?'

'I don't think there's a… um…' The word couldn't roll out of my mouth. It had taken on a new life.

'You don't think or you know?'

'I looked and…'

'… and you know?'

'I know there isn't one down there.'

'Right. By the way,' the voice said, now retreating from the door, fading, 'by the way, did you see the note on your door?'

'I did.'

'Great. See the fridge and feel free.'

What was I to feel free about? I looked up and could make out the shape of a pyramid on the ceiling. The light switch was on a side of the stairwell. I flicked it on, and saw that it was indeed a drawing of a pyramid with an inscription beneath: *We Are the Originals. We Are Still Here.*

'Are you there, Frank?'

'I am,' I answered and switched off the light.

'OK, here,' the voice said, and as the door opened, slowly, a pale hand, not the full body, emerged with the plunger. 'Here,' the voice said again, and a female voice added from somewhere deep in the room, 'Have fun, Frank.' Mystery solved. There were two of them: Edna and the man. I could hear a low humming sound in the background, like a group of people mumbling in prayers or meditation. The intense smell of incense was also present.

Pinching the tip of the plunger between my thumb and index, to maintain maximum distance between the now symbolic object and my person, I fled downstairs.

Later that night, I tried to imagine where Kabumba and the rest were. They certainly weren't fighting food poisoning and clogged toilets, or wondering if their landlady was or wasn't who she claimed to be. But it was all about the experience, wasn't it?

From my open window voices drifted in, loud, and soon there was music, equally loud and heavy. I drew aside the curtain and saw that it was coming from the car parked on the street, now surrounded by more people. What if I went out there and introduced myself, 'Hey, I'm Frank Jasper, a brother from Africa, newly arrived in your neighbourhood'? It was a fleeting thought, and I knew there was no way on this depressing earth that I would pull off a stunt like that. Something crashed upstairs. Edna. I remembered her note and went to the fridge. Beer. Lots of it. I took two cans and returned to my room.

It would take days before I officially met Edna and the man upstairs. One morning there was a gentle knock on the door. 'Just checking in.' Her voice was a half-whisper, with an air of indifference, as though what was said was part serious and part dismissible, as if her own words bored her. 'Everything OK?' She sounded so casual, as if it wasn't the first time that I was seeing her. And the voice at close range couldn't be more different from what I'd imagined, going by how I'd interpreted her texts and emails. Before I could answer she walked away towards the kitchen, muttering as she went. I saw that she was barefoot, wearing a pair of black boxers and a white sports bra.

I followed her to the kitchen, where she'd planted herself at the only window, looking out, talking as if speaking to someone outside. 'If the land could speak, if the sea could sing, if time had a voice...'

I wanted to turn around and go back to my room, but there was something about her, something enigmatic, that glued me to the spot.

When she turned, now smiling, I said, 'Edna, I'm glad we finally met.'

She ignored my remark and said, 'Sorry, I was just rehearsing a speech for an event coming up. Are you finding everything OK?'

'I am,' I said.

Footsteps behind me. I turned and saw a man of average height, naked, with thick black hair on his chest, spreading sideways and down. His beard, cone-shaped and full, hung off his chin like a hanging flower basket. Thick eyeglasses. Thick eyebrows. An abstracted figure; the image of someone given to too much abstract thought, whose world orbited outside the known world, never touching ground, never perching, but also not at home in the ether. He appeared to me, just looking at him, as someone who – like myself – did not crave conversation. Allen Small, he said to introduce himself, looking at a point just above my head. Mystery solved. His was the hand that offered me the plunger my first day there.

I would get to know them better. Allen, as I later learned, was struggling to hold his mind together. And even now, when I think back to my time there, I still pray and hope he's doing OK, that he's found the help he needs.

I recall one episode when Allen had a breakdown: the screaming and weeping, punctuated by long declarations of himself as an invisible guardian of 'the great tradition', the only road back to the very beginning of poetry. The walls shook as his voice rose and broke, as he cursed those whose 'poems corrupt the pure line'. Downstairs, in my room, I felt a combination of worry, sadness and empathy. He was a gifted poet.

Edna had shared that with me, and I'd confirmed it myself by looking up his work. I was sad that a brilliant mind was so tortured and disintegrating, that it had completely lost touch with reality, and I empathised because my mother had also struggled to hold her mind together. But I was worried that in his moment of weakness it was hate that filled his mind. I heard him mourning the death of culture in America, where 'monkeys and pigs now write poems and direct culture'. He wept for what he called the end of 'poetic order' and of 'thinking verse'. It broke my heart. 'I'm a poet,' he'd announced the first day I met him, in the kitchen. That he was working on a 'long sequence' and the lines were 'heavy in his balls', waiting to 'spill'. He said he'd been told that I was a writer, and smirked as if he doubted the fact himself.

From Edna I learned that Allen lived in Roslindale, and was a bit of an old-fashioned Formalist, the type who 'weaponised language and tradition to put other people down'. They'd known each other since their days at the historic Renaissance School in Boston. And they attended the same college, graduating the same year Allen published his first chapbook, which subsequently won the Warwick Prize.

After college he moved to New York to work for *The New Measure*, an old magazine that had launched the careers of many writers. Three years later, fearing he was losing his mind in New York – 'Couldn't stand that fucking beast,' he'd said to Edna – he came back to Boston and began a PhD in American studies.

He dropped out a year later and was, indeed, losing his mind. He would stay indoors for days, barely eating. His girlfriend of many years left him. But still he wrote, furiously, pouring whatever energy he had into his work. The poems were no longer finding homes in magazines. He did not understand why. He came up with the theory that the world wasn't ready for his type of poetry, for the great revival that he was championing.

On my part, I tried to understand how the socially and politically conscious Edna got along so well with Allen. 'In there, somewhere,' she said, 'is the same generous and kind Allen I've always known.' It still didn't answer my question. How could she be championing the rights of minorities and women and the environment and still be close friends with someone who did not see minorities as capable of producing or consuming culture? He obviously wasn't walking down the street lynching immigrants and 'POCs' but it must be hurtful to hear him dismissing them, even when those outbursts arose in moments of mental collapse. Her capacity to see him as two things in one was astonishing.

The morning after he broke down, Edna knocked on my door and asked if I could keep an eye on him. He was still asleep in her room upstairs. She was going to Chestnut Hill to see her parents.

Later that day, when I went upstairs to check on him, he was lying on the floor, naked, looking lifeless, surrounded by crumpled paper and notebooks.

I picked up a crumpled paper, straightened it, and saw what he'd scribbled, something in the shape of a poem, illegible, in red ink. I checked three more crumpled pages. The same thing. I picked up a notebook, and saw that he had sketched portraits of himself. Same portrait on every page, with few variations.

There's a sweet spot between sleep and wakefulness, a small rosy slice that one must enjoy before transitioning to deep sleep. This was where I saw myself, around ten o'clock my first night at Edna's. And for some reason I was conscious of being there, and was aware of my muscles relaxing, of a balmy feeling flowing from my temples to my toes. And then something strange began to happen. It started with a distant noise, rising and fading, like horses charging towards a target. I felt my legs moving, thrashing, my body rolling over, resisting wakefulness, but it was too late. My eyes were now open. No, it wasn't a thousand horses outside. Voices, drunken voices, were in the hallway. I got out of bed, tiptoed to the door, gingerly opened it, and the first thing that caught my attention was a note on the opposite door. *See Fridge, and Just Feel Free! Peace and Sunshine.* Guests! Edna hadn't said anything about new guests checking in. 'I fucking love the Red Sox,' someone shouted in the kitchen. Another tumbled into the bathroom. I could hear them throwing up, cheered on by their friends. Someone was in charge, and I could hear her telling the rest what to do. 'Just order the pizza already,' she said. Her voice was straight and sharp. I ignored them and assumed Edna had told them there was someone else on the same floor. I hoped they would quieten down eventually. But to be sure they knew I was there, I opened the door and went into the shared bathroom. I heard the woman's voice, 'What da fuck? I thought we had the entire floor to ourselves.' When I came out of the bathroom, she was at the door. 'Hey mister, we kinda rented the entire apartment to ourselves, not sure what you're doing here.' Standing shirtless at the bathroom door, I thought to myself: First day here and someone is already accusing me of trespassing. 'I stay here,' I finally said, 'I live here. Enjoy your night and don't worry about keeping me up.' I wasn't sure why I added the last line. I went to the kitchen for a can of beer. Saw her partners. They were so drunk they seemed to look at me with eyes slouched to their chins. My intervention lasted only until I was back in my room. They continued as they were, drinking until three in the morning. They were gone when I woke up at 7 a.m., leaving pizza boxes, empty cans and bottles of beer everywhere. It was a sight that irritated me but also triggered a feeling of homesickness. It took me back to my own room in Port Jumbo, when I was writing my novel, the nights drinking beer alone, each empty can squeezed and tossed to the same corner, the dense smell of stale beer that lingered for days, that I left to linger because it felt like another presence, became another presence, an invisible body that kept me company as I imagined the life of my protagonist, creating for him a world that could only exist in the mind of someone from my background.

That feeling of homesickness intensified as that period of my life came back to me. Frustrated, I took the train downtown, just to put my mind elsewhere. I found myself lingering around Washington Street, unsure where to go.

Turning left, eventually, on Broomfield Street, I headed on to Tremont.

At the intersection of Broomfield and Tremont, I saw a small shop that caught my attention, Eudora's Stamp Corner.

I went in and asked, 'Do you have stamps from West Africa?'

'Yes, we do, any country in particular?'

'Nigeria,' I said.

'I'm guessing you're Nigerian,' she said, sounding sure of it.

I detected a slight shift in her accent, from what I thought was a mild Southern accent to a wavering British inflection.

At the back wall of the little shop hung a print of François Barraud's *Le Philateliste* and at another end was a framed quote from a passage in Louis Aragon's *Paris Peasant*: 'O philately, philately: you are a most strange goddess.'

Looking through a huge leatherback folder containing stamps from Africa, she said, 'I had a Nigerian friend growing up.'

She stopped at a page that read at the top of it: NIGERIA/ GHANA.

She turned the folder in my direction. I'd seen most of the stamps before.

'A Nigerian friend here in Boston?' I asked.

'Oh, no,' she said. 'I grew up in Norwich, in the UK.'

She was born in Jackson, Mississippi, she said, but moved with her parents to Norwich in the late sixties when her father got a teaching job at the newly established University of East Anglia. She was just six then and lived there for twelve years before moving back for college at the Mississippi University for Women.

I told her about my job at the post office and mentioned how I'd picked up an interest in philately and started the first stamp collectors' club in Port Jumbo. The part about the club was a lie. But in that moment, homesick, not wanting to court or endure silence, I found myself making up stories to keep the conversation going, surprising myself. I further shocked myself by rambling on about Port Jumbo, the things I liked about it: the view of the ocean from the Eastern Promenade, the sight of boats coming and going, the constant noise (which I hated but in that moment began to miss). I talked about the Blue Plaque Project in Port Jumbo, an idea put forward by the current postmaster general to honour important citizens and foreigners who at one time or another had lived in or passed through the city. She seemed to listen. But I had a suspicion that she could see through me and knew I just needed the conversation.

There would be one plaque on a house on my street, I said, to mark where five American writers – Kurt Vonnegut, Herbert Gold, Harvey Swados, Leslie Fiedler, Vance Bourjaily – stayed at various times in the late sixties.

'Vonnegut was in Nigeria?'

'Yes,' I answered.

So, how did she end up in Boston?

Well, after college she returned to Norwich and got a job at the Norfolk Institute of Art and Design, but also worked on the weekends at a stamp collection shop not far from the cathedral. The owner was her boyfriend, a fellow American who was also the editor of *Stamp and Travel Magazine*.

When the magazine folded in the early nineties, and the shop was losing money, they moved back to the States, first to Rhode Island, and then to Boston.

A man walked in. Rough-looking, late middle age, a face nearly covered in hair. He stood next to me by the counter, standing a full inch taller. He interrupted the conversation, his voice booming, 'Has it arrived yet?'

Yes, *it* had arrived. She excused herself to browse through another thick folder on a desk near the back wall.

She came back with a set of stamps, placed them on the countertop, and he leaned forward, examining them closely.

I couldn't tell what the stamps were worth or where they came from.

'At last, at last,' the man said. Turning to me, he asked, 'Isn't she lovely, eh?'

I looked closely at the stamp, a profile of a young woman with the inscription *Province of Griqualand West*. I had no idea where Griqualand was or who the Griquas were. I asked, and the man, shooting me a sharp look, said, 'You are African, no? And you don't know about Griqualand?'

The woman said, 'He's from Nigeria, Paul.'

'Still,' the man said.

He clearly wasn't American, a fact I'd already picked up from his accent.

Shaken out of my mood by this encounter, I decided I'd had enough human interaction for one day.

An hour or so later, idling over a flat white at the Starbucks between Webster and Lepson, I saw the same man marching towards me. He'd seen me from the outside and decided to come say hello. Odd, I thought, but managed to summon some enthusiasm.

He went up to order, and I thought of escaping but waited.

'So, Nigerian, eh?' he asked when he returned with his cappuccino. 'What are you doing in Boston? Doing Harvard like your fellow Nigerians? They are obsessed with Harvard, no?'

'Harvard?' I asked. 'I'm not sure I'm the Harvard type.'

He showed no interest in what 'type' I was or wasn't.

'I'm a writer,' I shared, not exactly sure why I said it.

Being a Nigerian writer did not explain my presence in Boston, or in the United States for that matter. 'I'm with the writing programme at William Blake College,' I added to provide context.

When people hear you're a writer, someone once said, they tell you things, hoping you'll use their story in one of your books or poems, and by doing so fetch them a piece of immortality. The man's tongue loosened once he heard what I did. As he talked, I began to get the impression that he was battling with some internal conflict. He was born in Boston, he said, the Boston in the province of KwaZulu-Natal in South Africa. He began his career at the age of seventeen, working on a small farm outside Durban, after which he worked for a mining company for ten years before branching out to form his own company with operations in South Africa and Sierra Leone. It was that company that he'd recently sold. Now he was living the life he'd always wanted. First, he bought a boat and sailed from Durban to Zanzibar, and from there to Mombasa, where he traded his boat for a truck and drove inland to Nairobi. Then, he began his main quest: to travel around the world and see as many Bostons as possible. It was a childhood obsession, after learning that his home town of Boston in KwaZulu-Natal was not the only Boston out there.

His first stop was the Boston in Lincolnshire, UK, where he stayed at a guesthouse on the edge of *their* Central Park.

'You know,' he continued, 'in the first two hours I spent there, I didn't hear one word of English.'

The next day he went to St Botolph's Church. He pulled out his phone to show me photos. A sign outside St Botolph's read: PURITAN PATH. Another photo showed a list of St Botolph's congregation members who sailed to the New World in the fifteenth century: William Coddington, Thomas Leverett... and the Reverend Isaac Johnson, who 'sailed with his wife on the *Arbella* to Massachusetts Bay'. There was a close-up shot of the note under that Puritan Path: 'On the 8th of April 1630, prominent members of the Reverend John Cotton's congregation of St Botolph's Church set sail on board the *Arbella* for New England to establish the Massachusetts Bay Colony and to realise their Vision of founding a "City upon a Hill" under their chosen leader John Winthrop.'

The day after, he went to the Pilgrim Fathers Memorial. He showed me more pictures. There was nothing spectacular about the place or the memorial, which looked like a table bell resting on grass. I read the inscription at the base of it: 'Near this place in September 1607 those later known as the Pilgrim Fathers were thwarted in their first attempt to sail to find religious freedom across the seas.'

As I continued to scroll through photos, he said he'd recently gone to see the Pilgrim Monument 'here' in Provincetown, and mentioned how he climbed up the monument, through its interior, up the steps and ramps, until he stood and surveyed the area as far as the eye could see. It reminded him of climbing the tower at St Botolph's Church 'over there across the pond', where, as he recalled, the inside walls of the tower were covered in inscriptions going back decades: students marking years of graduation, friends immortalising friends, lovers leaving traces of their love.

I finished my coffee and said I was going outside for a smoke.

'I haven't smoked in years,' he said.

I offered him one. He accepted.

Outside, a young couple in matching sweatshirts with their baby, the man pushing the stroller, squinted at us. A grey Volkswagen Beetle pulled up, forcing everyone around to turn and look at this little time capsule. 'Muslims Are Not Terrorists', a sticker screamed from the rear windshield.

'So where are you off to next?' I asked.

'Boston, Ontario,' he said, a hint of excitement in his voice. He asked: 'Have you written anything that I can read?'

Hesitating, I caved. 'Yes, a novel.'

'Is it available online?'

What could I say – *it* was available somewhere on the internet. 'Yes,' I said, 'it's called *The Day They Came for Dan*.'

'Great. Your name again?'

'Frank Jasper.'

'Jasper? Interesting,' he said. 'You're the second Jasper I've met this week. Well,' he added, 'the other Jasper was a British suffragette who lived in Providence under a different name many years ago. One Hilary, or was it Harriet? There's an exhibition about her at the Providence Athenæum.'

My heart skipped a beat as he mentioned her name. Could it be the same Harriet Jasper, she who stole my great-grandfather's heart? The chances were slim. But there was a chance.

Staying calm, I said I had someplace to go.

I wished him well on his journey.

I looked up the exhibition, read the summary, and there was no doubt about it: it was her.

I ran to the station downtown and caught an afternoon train to Providence. For the first time in years I felt a surge of meaning and purpose. I said to myself, this may be the real reason why I'm in the US, to be reconnected with a part of my past that was out there somewhere in the world. And this feeling intensified when I arrived in Providence, at the Athenæum, and saw her name on the exhibition leaflet: *Major Lives in the Margins: On Florence Anthony and Anne Bower (Harriet Jasper).*

There was also a book by one Cara Moore, the curator, a professor at King's College London and visiting researcher at the Athenæum.

I bought the book. I held it close to my chest, feeling its weight. I flipped through pages with black and white photographs of Harriet as a child, as a young woman, of her childhood home in Hertfordshire, of the house where she lived for a while in London.

And there was a drawing from the late nineteenth century showing Lairdstown on the edge of the River Niger, pairing that world of colonial Nigeria with the one she knew in England and the one in Providence where she chose to live out the rest of her life.

A section of Moore's book provided details about Harriet's life at St Mary's Refuge in Tavistock, the home for unwed mothers where her father had sent her. The Sisters there found her 'irritable', the book said. They described her as a trouble-maker, and they kept her away from books and isolated her. At night she would scream into the void, as if to call forth a force to rescue her. At dawn she would recoil into herself, refusing food, refusing life itself. What was the point of going on, of holding on to life, when nothing made sense, when the child inside her was already marked as an outsider, sold in advance to whoever was interested in an interracial child? What was the point of going on when there wasn't even room to question anything, when questioning was itself a sign that one was a problem?

When the baby came, it was given away to a wealthy American family from New York. They sold my child, she would later write.

She knew her daughter was out there in America. Where exactly in America, she did not know. She would later move to that country, crossing the ocean as her daughter had done. She wanted to stay close to her, to be comforted by the thought of breathing the same American air as the child who had been taken away from her.

The exhibition itself, displayed in a small corner of the Athenæum, consisted of photographs, letters, posters, news-paper cuttings and books from the archives of Florence and Harriet held at the Athenæum. One could go around the corner and back again in forty minutes. I stayed for two hours, stud-ying each object, looking into her face, our Harriet, as each photograph showed the calm face of a woman whose name never left the lips of my ancestors.

Both women, as pictures revealed, were fond of smoking fat cigars in public, and enjoyed hosting large parties at Florence's house, the mansion her parents built in Providence. In one photo, a party scene, an unidentified man was lighting Florence's cigar while Harriet looked on.

They were active in the local Suffrage Union, and in one case, after a demonstration, they were arrested and Harriet was nearly deported, rescued eventually by the intervention of Florence's uncle, a law professor at Yale.

Standing in front of a portrait of Harriet by a prominent Providence painter, I waited for something to communicate itself, for an explanation as to why she chose to burst into my consciousness here in the US. The more I waited – studying her jawline, the unwavering certainty in her eyes, her long black hair – the more real she became. I moved closer, touched her forehead. I listened for her voice to speak to me across the vast century between us. I closed my eyes, listening to the silence that separated but also united us.

The part of the story I wasn't following, as I moved along from one piece to another, was how the transformation had happened, how the religious Harriet had lost her faith and found a new form of freedom. That piece of the puzzle was resolved, to some extent, by a change-of-name document on display. When she left St Mary's after the birth of her child, she changed her name from Harriet Jasper to Anne Bower and began a new life in London, a young woman alone.

In London, she carried on thinking about her brief but passionate encounter with love in Africa, an experience that altered everything about her. She wondered what became of the father of her child, if he was still holding on to a faith that denied him love. She wrote a short novel under her new name. The story of an English girl in love with a boy in Africa. *What the River Gave* was never published. The manuscript survived, and was now in preparation for publication with an introduction by Cara Moore.

There were excerpts in Cara's book, including the scene where the narrator and her lover (my great-grandfather) slipped out in the middle of a moonlit night and hiked the narrow road leading to the very top of Mount Patti, defying instructions to stay away from that spot. She (Harriet) wanted to see the River Niger illuminated at night, and she described it as a resting snake glowing under the African moon. A later novel, also unpublished, was more critical of that phase of her life, of her unintended role in a broader project of exploitation and cultural erasure.

A docent walked in and saw me standing too close to a notebook that belonged to Florence Anthony, the page opened to an unfinished poem. The docent came close, stood behind me and, as if struck by a change of mind, walked away, not without shooting me an inquisitive look, as if to say, 'What could this possibly mean to you?'

Unsure how I would answer if her lips had spoken what her eyes said, I moved on to the next object, a series of missing-person advertisements in London newspapers, placed by Harriet's family.

In one ad, her parents said she was a sleepwalker who left the house one night and never came back. They gave her height, the colour of her eyes and hair. A reward awaited anyone with useful information on the whereabouts of Harriet Jasper. And so the world swung into action, searching for Miss Jasper, who no longer existed.

While they were looking for her, she was planning her journey to America.

That summer, in London, she met Florence Anthony and her husband, the biographer James Fosdick, who was then at work on his now famous study of the Fireside Poets. Married only two years, the couple were in London visiting friends and giving talks.

Harriet, now going as Anne, was present at Florence's talk on Amy Lowell, held at Gordon Hall. The women were not far apart in age, Florence being only two years older. Theirs was an 'instant bond', as Cara's book mentioned, a bond forged by a mutual interest in Lowell. Harriet had also read the two volumes of verse Florence had published, one of which Yeats himself endorsed.

While Fosdick traversed London discussing John Whittier and William Bryant, Florence and Harriet visited galleries and museums. When Harriet mentioned her plan to move to the US, Florence offered to put her up. She could stay as long as she wanted, and that was what happened when Harriet arrived in Providence. The next year, both women took a trip to Scotland, and then Europe, bypassing London.

In Edinburgh they met John Morgan, the Scottish poet and educator, who Florence knew. Morgan had just returned from Port Jumbo, where he was starting up a school for boys. Harriet did not mention her time in Africa – not to Morgan, not even to Florence. Morgan would return to Port Jumbo a year later, and would meet my great-grandfather, Harriet's lover.

Back in Providence, Harriet and Florence met an empty house. Fosdick had moved out, going up north to New Hampshire. He was silent about the reason for the move. It was now the two women alone and they embarked on a lifelong companionship that drew attention from all quarters. After their deaths, their lives and works and activities disappeared from public conversation. It was only recently that writers and academics were beginning to rediscover Florence's work and map her relationship with Harriet.

In a corner, I saw the current edition of *The New Commentary*. It was open and folded to a page with an article about the exhibition. The writer mentioned my great-grandfather and quoted an interview Moore had given a while back, where she talked about the similarities between Harriet's progressive politics and my great-grandfather's practices as an educator in colonial Nigeria. On the way out, I saw someone who looked like the curator. I wanted to walk over and introduce myself but I didn't.

On the train back to Boston, I wondered who to call or email to share my experience. My father, who just before his death renewed his interest in Harriet's life, would have leapt for joy. This would have been his moment, I thought, and would have given him something to be happy about as his life deteriorated, his lungs yielding to cancer.

Sometimes I regret that I judged my father too harshly, that I blamed my own inadequacies on the life he and my mother chose for themselves. The consequence of that was how little

I knew him as a person, as another human being, not just as the man I wanted to be different from.

When the committee kicked me out of the programme, I thought of my father again and how he would have laughed and shared one of his misadventures to make me feel better about myself. On that day, as the dean's solemn voice followed me around the streets of Boston, pressing its moral case and reminding me of how I had squandered a significant opportunity, I pictured my father on his favourite couch to the right of the main door, wearing the same robe he'd owned since his school days in the UK, the robe 'Francis gave me for my birthday'. That line came back to me as I walked through Boston without any destination in mind. I knew he was referring to Francis Bacon, the artist, and the occasion was his birthday party at the Colony Room in Soho, hosted by Ian Board, who was running the place after the death of its original owner, Muriel Belcher. For a moment I tried to imagine the world as he saw it, and how – unlike myself – he never paused to indulge any single emotion, always jumping from one mood to another, somehow managing to sustain a sense of equilibrium.

The closest person to my father's world before I was born was his American friend, Gerard Hopkins. I reached out to him, as I walked around the city, after leaving the dean and his committee. 'Except for the years I spent in England in the late seventies and eighties,' he said, 'I've lived here in Cherry Springs most of my adult life.' I could visit any time I wanted, he said. 'You are my godson after all,' he added, reminding me of a fact that heightened my curiosity to understand his relationship with my father.

I knew that Gerard had been present at my christening back in Nigeria, the only time he visited my father in Port Jumbo. That was all I knew about him, outside the little I gathered from his letters to my father dating back to their time in the UK, and the basic facts my father shared one afternoon, after a long phone call with Gerard, who had just undergone cataract surgery.

The image of Gerard in my head was the one from a photograph at my christening, which wasn't really a christening since my parents didn't believe in anything. In the picture, he's holding me and peering at me, his monstrous beard a hair away from my face, the large collars of his floral shirt hanging like flappy dog ears.

I once looked him up online and saw nothing but a single article from the archives of *The New York Compass*, a short-lived anti-war magazine published in the late seventies by a group of American students living in Paris. It was an essay on J.M. Coetzee's *Dusklands*, published in 1974, and in just a few paragraphs the piece attacked what it considered 'the collapse of our capacity to feel and empathise'. The tone was that of a writer who was politically active, which came as a surprise to me since the Gerard in my head, as a friend of my pleasure-for-pleasure's-sake father, was indifferent to such matters.

I once asked my father how he met Gerard and why Gerard had the same name as the poet whose collected works was among the volumes that he, my father, occasionally pulled out and read. He responded with poetry, as he always did when he wanted to evade a subject. From the poet Gerard Manley Hopkins, he quoted: 'With witness I speak this. But where I say / Hours I mean years, mean life. And my lament / Is cries countless, cries like dead letters sent / To dearest him that lives alas! away.' My mother, overhearing, laughed and responded, 'Oh shut up and answer the boy's question.'

'Let's start with the name,' my father began, 'Gerard Hopkins. Named after the English poet. His father was an Englishman who followed his American wife back to the US, to Pulaski, somewhere in the Midwest – named after some Polish chap.'

And Dad digressed and spent the entire afternoon talking about Casimir Pulaski, how Pulaski served under General Washington during the American Civil War, 'saving Washington's life on one occasion'. And we never got around to finishing the conversation about his friend.

What I gathered years later, from one of my father's many diary entries, where he meticulously kept notes of everything he saw and experienced abroad and at home, was that Gerard's mother was a black jazz singer in London just after the war, and Gerard's father, who had fallen out with his wealthy English family, was the young owner of a club in Leicester Square, where Gerard's mother sang. Gerard had shared this detail with my father a week after they met. 'I thought Gerard was a white boy,' Dad wrote in his diary. No further entries on the subject.

■

Three days after the committee reached its decision, I found myself on the road to Cherry Springs in Nebraska to see Gerard, running away from the site of my disgrace, drawn to the possibility of a new discovery about my father and about myself.

14

I T was somewhere between Iowa and Nebraska, forced off the highway by a heavy downpour, trapped in my car in front of the Midcountry Chicken & Fries, a fast-food outlet that looked like it could use a facelift, that I began to feel my own presence in the middle of America. I had no signal on my phone. The rain was showing no sign of abating. And I had no idea where I was.

There was a gas station to my left, thirty-five-odd yards away, and beyond that the edge of a cornfield, or what looked like a cornfield.

The sound of the rain, monotonous and hypnotic, became the sound of memory, replaying my time in Boston and the chain of events that brought me to America.

I heard Perky's voice, soft but firm in its reproach. 'You blew it, Frank, you blew it big time.' She'd slammed the trunk of her car after saying this, watching me transfer my suitcase to the red Prius at the Avis car rental on Mass Avenue, where she was dropping me off. I wondered out loud how I'd blown it, to which, folding her arms across her breasts and leaning back on the trunk of her car, she responded in a sharp voice, 'That's the problem, Frank, you can't seem to get outside your head.'

'How do you mean?' I asked, looking her in the eye for the first time since leaving her house that morning. She did not answer. Instead she sighed and shook her head. Then she fished out a brown Manila envelope, handed it to me, and gave me a long hug.

I tried to force Perky off my mind by straining to see the shape of three wind turbines to my right, their expansive blades almost fading into haze and low clouds, rotating slowly but effectively through empty space.

Cars pulling in and leaving. Middle Americans entering and exiting the fast-food outlet. I, too, needed to go inside for lunch. I was starving. The thought of starving to death in the centre of America's corn belt amused me.

For some reason, I guess it was the thought of corn, I recalled a documentary I had seen many years earlier, about Khrushchev's visit to Roswell Garst's farm in Coon Rapids, Iowa, how both men bonded over that great crop, how ordinary farmers and locals, outside the volcanic hotness of Cold War politics, came out en masse to see the Russian leader.

I was so lost in my corn fantasies that I didn't hear the sound of someone knocking on the trunk of my car. The rain was still falling, pounding harder and harder. I thought the sound was coming from the inside of my car, perhaps something installed by the rental company to remind me of a problem with the engine. Then I assumed it was the echo from a car door slamming shut over at the gas station. But it grew louder, repeating itself, a series of *bang, bang, bang*s with smaller bangs in-between.

Alarmed, I looked back but could not make out what it was.

I saw a shape, blurred by the rain, towering behind.

And then it banged again, once, walked around to the passenger side, and tapped on the window. There it was, a broad-shouldered man in a worn army raincoat, smiling and knocking and demanding attention.

Looking at him – the missing front teeth, the sunken eyes, the tufted hair from his broad nostrils – I felt trapped and obliged to be nice. Besides, he was a 'brother', and I could see him mouthing it, 'Brother, please…' with his head cocked to one side, and with the stupid rain now a drizzle we were both in full view, with the staff at the Midcountry Chicken & Fries able to see us through the wide window.

I thought to myself, if this was the streets of Port Jumbo, or anywhere in Nigeria, I would have done one of two things without feeling any type of 'brotherly' guilt, or worry that I might be reinforcing or perpetuating or breaking any 'brotherly' code: I'd either frown and ignore him, or yell something like, 'My man, the country no good, no money,' at which the beggar would leave or reply with a string of insults. It was a game of mutual loathing played by the down-and-out against the down-and-out, without recourse to some abstract ideology or morality. But here in the heart of America, in a space where we were the only 'black bodies', I felt like I needed to respond to a 'brother', to perform a humane gesture.

For a moment I had a feeling he knew what he was doing. I thought I saw a twinkle in his eyes, as if he was saying, 'Ha, you better be brotherly or…'

And to make things worse he had a small cardboard sign that announced his status as a veteran: FOUGHT FOR THE UNITED STATES.

So I raised my palm to plead for patience. I mouthed, 'Wait, I'll give you something.'

He waved to decline, and mouthed a reply, 'No, I don't want your money,' and gestured towards the entrance to the Midcountry Chicken & Fries.

He wanted lunch and was firm about it.

I pictured the growing sea of eyes, watching, curious.

Ahead, I saw a plump fellow in cargo trousers at the entrance to the Midcountry Chicken & Fries fiddling with his wallet, or pretending to do so, casting us quick glances. I had seen him earlier on when he pulled up in a white utility van and spent a minute or two considering us, squinting, unable to conceal his concern. The 'brother' and I were already a spectacle in the corn belt, in a place where, in my mind, there was little or no drama besides farm animals escaping captivity. The presence of two curious figures was enough spectacle, with the potential to spin into a tale that would resound and retell itself for years to come.

Again, I raised my palm. He gestured to press his point: he wanted me to buy him lunch.

I squeezed out a smile.

I performed hospitality.

I could sense his satisfaction at my defeat.

I stepped out of the car and inhaled the fresh smell of the wet open fields nearby.

I took another deep breath and offered a contrived smile.

I noticed that the smell of the open fields had been displaced by a violent odour that was hard to place. For a second the open sewers of Port Jumbo, their contents overflowing, flashed before me. I shuddered and repressed the memory.

I offered him a handshake. The texture of his palm was coarse as sandpaper, and his stone-solid grip, almost crushing my vegetable-soft palm, struck me as an attempt to humiliate me.

'Firm handshake,' I mumbled and repeated my contrived smile.

'Thank you,' he said, and cackled as though I'd said something funny.

I ignored his laughter and pointed to the door, where I saw a couple entering, the man awkwardly holding the door for a woman who seemed to hesitate, as if to say, 'Gee, thanks, but I was going for the knob.'

The stranger made no attempt to move, to follow my hint. He had stopped laughing. And now, as if on cue, he steadied his gaze, holding my eyes with his.

If the eyes are windows to the soul, his were gateways that led nowhere. What you saw was all you got.

We were almost the same height, but his wild hair gave him an extra inch or two. And his longish face, in contrast to my squarish head, created the illusion that he was taller.

I spotted a small, almost invisible scar above his left eye, between his brow and lid, that made it look like he was winking. I averted my gaze and began to walk towards the entrance to the Midcountry Chicken & Fries, hoping he would follow me and that after lunch he would go his own way and leave me to go mine.

I'll regret this, I said to myself, a few paces ahead of him.

At the entrance, I turned to see him standing where I left him, his eyes on me, his mouth drawn as if a sneer was brewing.

It was warm inside the Midcountry Chicken & Fries. The walls to the left, right and back were painted white, changing to yellow on the other side of the counter. The counter was red except for the wooden surface. The entire space was smaller than I had thought. No windows except the wide rectangular glass by the entrance.

With just a few tables arranged against the walls, leaving room only between the counter and the entrance, I saw myself standing in the centre, bare and vulnerable. I tried to read the badly calligraphed menu above the counter.

I approached the two staff, one slender and the other not-quite-slender, both motionless, standing side by side.

'I'll have a veggie burger,' I said, and the slender one, breaking her blank face with a grin, responded, 'Oh, honey, we've not had those in months, you know, they're not popular around here.'

I took stock of everyone I had seen so far and I agreed with her.

I re-examined the meat-centric menu. 'The cheeseburgers look good,' a flat voice spoke, just inches away from the back of my head. 'I'll have one,' he added. I turned and it was my man standing there, holding his oversized raincoat.

'A cheeseburger?' the not-quite-slender one asked.

I sensed a sharpness to her voice, a marked difference from the sweet ring of her colleague's response to my order. I was relieved to know that they saw the difference between us, that

I was the real customer and my man, now inching forward to stand beside me, was an unwanted appendage.

I suppressed the rising guilt in me.

I took another step back and gave him a full look.

He was in good shape. A full head of hair with only dots of grey. How old was he? His navy-blue shirt had a wide hole on the left shoulder, baring skin as black as mine. I looked down to where his worn army trousers were tucked into military boots caked in mud. I wondered where those boots had been. Some field in that corner of the corn belt, where he helped out on a farm? Some village in Asia, if truly he 'fought for the United States'? The possibility of finding out over lunch temporarily diluted the growing anxiety of sharing a table with him.

'And for you, sir?'

'I'll have the same,' I answered.

'Two cheeseburgers, fries.' She wondered if we were 'together or paying separately'.

'We're together,' I said, stressing *together* with an air of brotherliness. I handed her a ten-dollar bill with an exaggerated air of being in charge of the unfolding scene.

'I'll have your orders ready,' she said in a neutral voice and disappeared through the door behind her.

I turned around to see that my strange companion had retreated from the counter and planted himself at a stool by the window, elbows on the ledge, rubbing his palms together and looking out as if to take stock of everything out there.

Looking beyond him, I saw a truck pulling in to the gas station.

I stole my gaze away from him and the window, lingered at the counter, and pretended to look through the selection of beverages.

'I can tell you're not from around here.' It was the slender one, Nicole, as her name tag said. There was certainty in her voice. There is no way, I imagined her thinking, that *he* is from around here.

'I'm not,' I answered. 'I'm on my way to Colorado,' I lied.

'Neat,' she said. 'It's beautiful out there.' She said this in the voice of those who have perfected the art of apathetic chatter. 'I have family up there,' she added for good measure.

'Oh, where?'

'In Lawrence,' she said, and shared more about Lawrence and how it was now 'part of the greater Boulder' area but used to be 'very distinct and different' back in the day, with more 'charm and character', without the new 'fancy restaurants' and the 'California transplants' and so on and so forth.

Her careful choice of words and the sequence in which she said them surprised me. I resisted the urge to share how impressed I was, how unexpected her articulacy was considering where she was from. In a slow fashion that again caught me off guard, she brushed back a strand of blonde hair straying from a corner of her red Midcountry Chicken hat. She asked, 'So, where in Colorado?'

'Palisade,' I said, dropping the name of a town I had read about in a book years ago.

'Never been but I've heard good things. Any family there?'

'Oh no, just going to work on a peach orchard for a few weeks.'

'You'll like it down there,' she said, 'it's pretty this time of year.'

I sensed a warm undertone this time, a hint of sincerity, a departure from the practised disinterest of small talk. Maybe it was the mention of working at a peach farm. Some kind of working-class solidarity? The cheeseburgers appeared and I didn't get the chance to gauge where the warmth in her voice was coming from.

I sat next to the stranger, suddenly feeling so self-conscious that I couldn't touch my burger. I could sense all the eyes looking at us. And that distinct smell of stale urine and unwashed flesh was present, coming from him. He was also hesitating to eat.

Instead, he unscrewed the cap on a bottle of Mountain Dew that he'd picked from the fridge. The loud escape of gas startled me and intensified my sensitivity to the eyes around us. I looked around and noticed how quiet the place had become. The steady hum of kitchen machinery and the occasional shuffle of feet from the handful of seated customers faded into the background, outdone now by the loud *glup*, *glup*, *glup* sound of Mountain Dew going down his throat. The radio, which had been bleating country tunes, had for some reason gone silent.

I finally divided my burger into equal halves to ease the stress of handling the horrendous mass of beef between the buns. I picked the left half and bit with care.

'You're making a mess, son.' He spoke without looking at me. I was indeed making a mess. The grease was all over the place. The meat was sliding out of the bun. A ring of onion had escaped onto my lap.

'So, you were in Afghanistan?' I asked, just to change the topic, picking up the ketchup-stained onion ring.

'Iraq,' he answered, 'different country.'

'Of course.'

'It fucks with your head, you know, war and all that shit.'

He had raised his voice a bit, enough for the good customers around to hear the last word. I tilted my head away from him, took stock of our environment, and returned to the second half of my burger.

The silence around us intensified. A ripple of panic ran down my spine. A unique kind of panic, different from the fear of a looming physical attack. The heightened consciousness of being watched.

'Are you OK, son?'

There was a kind of certainty in his voice. It made me uneasy. Son? He could be my father all right, but why perform a familial bond with a total stranger?

I'm not OK, I wanted to say, but I remained silent. I also wished I could ask how he managed to stay calm, composed and sure of himself in a place like that, where folks did not hide their curiosity but instead inflicted it on their object of interest. I, for one, could not wait for it to be over, to leap out the door and hit the highway.

I thought of following up on the thing about war and how it fucked with your head. Maybe start one of those little talks about the invasion of Iraq, the politics involved, those who benefited from that war, and those whose daily lives were shattered and altered forever. But I knew nothing about the specifics of that war and had only followed reports of the looting of the National Museum of Iraq. I recalled getting a kick out of the image of a stolen sacred vase that was recovered in the profane trunk of a car in Baghdad. But bringing that up might be a waste of time, I thought.

A couple walked in, holding hands. Twenty-one at most. They were incredibly fit, both with long black hair, in matching black pants. I could see their yellow van outside, with a Nebraska licence plate.

'I'll be back in a second,' I said to him and headed to the restroom.

I wanted to be alone.

I closed the toilet lid and sat on it, looking at the door, reading the inscriptions and drawings left by previous users.

Just as I began to study those inscriptions, to distract myself by figuring out what they were, I heard a loud crash followed by gasps and the disordered movement of feet.

'Call 911,' I heard someone say. 'Call an ambulance,' the voice continued, and asked, 'Where's his friend?'

I lingered to catch my breath, and when I emerged I saw the stranger on the floor, motionless, both legs stretched out evenly and head tilted to the side, right arm akimbo, left arm tucked in by his side, a small circle of white observers peering into his face.

15

I T was the fellow in cargo trousers who made the first move, breaking from the circle of onlookers and dashing out the door. The young couple and the two waitresses, standing at all angles around the stranger like tourists catching the last act of a street juggler, began to talk among themselves. Was he from around here? Had anyone seen him here before? The closest hospital was twenty-five miles away; should they drive him there or wait for an ambulance? Probably best to drive him there – but wait, what about his friend? Could he be his son, maybe his brother? It was at this point, about three minutes after I'd come out of the restroom and seen the whole scene, that I inched towards the stranger on the floor.

Someone asked, 'Are you two together?'

'Oh, no,' I answered, 'I just bought him lunch.'

There was a short pause, as if they all wanted me to say more, to explain myself, to contextualise my exotic accent and my relationship with the man on the floor, who could easily pass as my father or uncle. After all, we were the only black figures in that small space.

To my relief, the door swung open and the man in cargo

trousers tumbled back inside with a CPR kit, panting as though he'd run a marathon.

'Is he breathing?' he inquired between his own short breaths, and without waiting for answers he shoved us aside and knelt beside the stranger. 'Did anyone get hold of an ambulance?'

'Not yet,' said Nicole, the waitress, 'the connection is terrible.'

It was raining again. The man placed his ears on the stranger's chest. 'He's alive,' he said. 'But we need to get him to the hospital. My van is loaded with tools and junk. We could unload but if anybody wants to volunteer their car...'

He rose to his feet and met my eyes. I turned to the couple standing next to me. They looked at each other in contrived confusion.

I volunteered to drive him to the hospital. Nicole offered to go with us.

I and the man in cargo shorts, who introduced himself as Jeff, lifted the stranger, who at this very minute peed himself, each sad drop trailing us as we carried him to the car, where he slumped in the back seat, almost lifeless. Nicole sat in front. We tore off onto the dirt road, dispersing puddles as we headed out towards the highway.

'I know where we're going,' Nicole said when I pulled out my phone and asked for an address. 'Take the first exit,' she said, 'it's coming up in five minutes or so.' She followed up with a line that I didn't care to engage, something about the bad reception 'around here' and how it reminded her of a time when 'folks' knew how to get around without phones.

The stranger, still unconscious, was propped up and supported by Jeff who was now going through the stranger's pockets, as Nicole suggested, to find any form of identification.

We drove up a small hill, farther away from the highway, and descended towards a handful of houses arranged on both sides of the road, with small lawns out front – an American flag here, and over there a yard sign displaying the name of a candidate running for office. More flags of various sizes: draped above doors, standing alone on poles, fluttering above rooftops, planted in a row on front lawns. I'd never seen so many flags in one small corner of any town or neighbourhood.

We passed a billboard alerting us to the nearness of a gas station, food mart and hospital, noting their respective distances away. A giant water tank, towering high on spindly legs, announced the name of the town as Clayton.

'No cell phone on him,' Jeff said. 'Receipts, more receipts, two Amtrak tickets… and what do we have here? A pocket notebook with numbers and addresses, a good sign.'

'A good sign,' I repeated quietly, conscious of my foreign accent and somewhat indifferent to the unfolding scene. All I wanted was to deliver our stranger to the hospital and be done with the whole nightmare. But part of me paid attention, sensing the unfolding incident might brew into a story, a book, or just lead to a clearer understanding of some aspect of American life.

We crossed a small bridge, passed a yard sale on the side of the road, where a couple stood next to a green pickup truck. Nicole untied her hair and ran her fingers through it.

I peered into the rear-view mirror. Jeff was speaking: 'There's a number for someone called Francesca Brooks and another one for a daughter in Chicago.' He coughed for what seemed a lifetime and continued: 'There's also a number for a son in Des Moines. And it says here, "If found return to Henry Tanner." No address, though.'

The stranger now had a name. Henry Tanner. And from the pocket notebook we learned that he may have lived in Chicago, as between the pages there were old passes to see exhibitions at the Art Institute of Chicago. This made me wonder if he was an artist, if he had exhibited work some-where, made his name in some small circle before taking a more practical path joining the army, if he really had been in the army.

We couldn't reach the Chicago and Des Moines numbers. We tried Francesca Brooks.

She picked up and confirmed that she knew him.

She was his ex-wife and she lived in Victor, just outside Grinnell, and said she would drive out to meet us.

Waiting for Francesca to arrive, surrounded by families waiting for updates about loved ones, Nicole revived the conversation we began at the Midcountry Chicken & Fries, about her visits to Colorado. She used to go up there in the summer to see her family. She was much younger then, she said, and her older cousins would drive her around Lawrence and she would fix her eyes on the horizon, tracking the shape of the mountains.

I listened. Her words came fully formed, like short poems, capturing her memories in concrete detail. I could almost see and touch and smell the landscape she described. I could see the white residue of snow in the distant mountains. And at sundown, she said, the mountains would take the form of a long line of squatting camels. Such lush descriptions, coming from a roadside waitress. The wonders of the United States. Then it struck me how much she knew and talked about the land, how much emotion she poured into her description, she of Swedish descent – as she mentioned – whose family 'came here' just before World War I. How, I thought, did she become so close to a land that had its own pulse and soul long before her ancestors arrived?

The door swung open. A woman dressed and looking like Condoleezza Rice walked in and introduced herself. It was Francesca.

Seeing her, the strand of silver hair resting against her left temple, the TV-ready face, I began to wonder what events in the past conspired to match her with the stranger. How and where did Mr Tanner meet his Condoleezza?

I followed her with my eyes as she took charge on arrival, making sure papers were signed, going through the ritual: insurance details, identity checks, relationships and whatnot.

She came over and thanked us, and to clear things up she said a few words about Mr Tanner. His real name was Patrick McHenry, the father of two veterans of the more recent war in Iraq, himself a veteran of the Gulf War. He never fully recovered from the mental torture it inflicted on him. Whenever he experienced a breakdown, which had become too frequent, he would take on the identities of his sons, Henry and Tanner, mixing up his Iraq with theirs, and would leave his place in Des Moines, travelling alone, supposedly looking for her.

It was a moving story, what war could do to the mind, yanking it away from reason, from coherence. I imagined there were hundreds, if not thousands, of 'Henry Tanners' roaming the corn belt and beyond, like ghosts in search of their former selves.

We left the hospital in Clayton around 6 p.m. After dropping off the others who had accompanied me, I drove for two hours to Conway, between Van Meter and De Soto, where I spent the night in an Airbnb that turned out to be someone's house converted into a hostel, not an actual spare room in a home as described on the website. The room itself, sparsely furnished and white, with a single bed, was on the top floor of a two-storey building.

It was already dark when I checked in. I showered and dined on two bags of Doritos and got into bed. I tried to relax but kept thinking about the stranger. I couldn't shake off the sight of his body stretched out on the floor at the Midcountry Chicken & Fries.

At some point my thoughts drifted to the day my father died. I remembered walking down the street leading to the hospital to see him, and feeling something heavy and strange, as if a part of my mind was detaching itself from the whole, floating away and above, leaving me incomplete and unbalanced.

When I entered the hospital and walked into his room and saw that it was empty, that feeling of incompleteness intensified, and I stood by the door looking at the well-made bed, trying to picture him there the way I had seen him last, his emaciated body, the motion his fingers made as he laboured to move them, and the way he turned to the window to avoid my eyes.

I went to the bed and sat facing the door, as if waiting for him to stroll in, and the tears began to stream down. I felt the weight of my heart, the loss, the sharp awareness that even though ours wasn't the father–son relationship I desired, it nonetheless meant something to me.

My mind drifted again to the stranger and I found myself praying for his quick recovery.

I fell asleep just before midnight.

Waking up, I heard voices seeping through the walls of my room. It was the couple next door who, last night, had been in a good mood, chatting and laughing, but at 6 a.m. were at each other's throats. 'She's my daughter,' the woman screamed, 'and you have no fucking right to talk about her like that,' to which the man replied, 'Doesn't change the fact that she's making the wrong decisions.'

It was a short-lived fight, but it woke me up, just in time for them to switch back to what they were: two companions, whispering and laughing together.

I reached for the side lamp in the dark but accidentally reached too far and knocked it over and it crashed across the room. There was a sudden hush on the other side of the wall. The couple had finally acknowledged my presence.

Feeling triumphant, I wondered if I should go for an early walk down the dirt road outside, taking up a standing offer made by the housekeeper to feel free to explore the grounds.

A leisurely stroll between the cornfields, careful not to trample on drops of fresh or caked cattle excrement, careful not to erase the precious footprints of deer and rodents. But I had a feeling the housekeeper had not meant what he said.

I thought of emailing Perky but pushed that thought aside. What had she put in the brown envelope she gave me? I was curious to know but had resisted the urge to open it. It was there in my suitcase, a silent voice chanting its demand to be heard. I imagined it contained farewell notes from my fellow writers on the William Blake programme, they whose presence made my lack of productivity even more glaring.

Just thinking about them and how active they were – organising events, mentoring undergraduates, blogging about their experiences in America – made my stomach ache. Kabumba was the most productive. I would ordinarily not expect a note from him. He could not stand the sight of me. But if farewell notes were in Perky's brown envelope, I would not be surprised to see something from him, at least a line or two. He was that sort of person – the guy who chipped in to ensure he played his part, who made a point to do his bit even when he could simply refuse on the grounds that he disapproved of the project.

Sara Chakraborty, on the other hand, would refuse to write me a note, and I would not be surprised if she started a long Twitter thread on how 'we need to start talking about the toxicity and entitlement of a certain kind of post-colonial Black man whose individual actions routinely sabotage the work' folks like her do to uplift 'people of colour'.

∎

Later, still in bed, I heard gunshots in the distance. Too distant to make me panic. A lone hunter? A shooting range? I went to the window, cracked it open. A wave of hot air eased in, and it felt good. More gunshots. I raised my eyes to survey the spaces ahead. Nothing out of the ordinary. Just the same expanse of green and brown with a series of paths running from one end of the cornfield to the other, and barns standing like small islands.

As if in response to the gunshots, someone jumped on the piano downstairs – I didn't know there was one – and I could hear them fingering away, an odd transition, I thought, from the sound of violence to the serenity of music. The wonders and intrigues of the corn belt. I knew what they were playing down there, with some difficulty, pausing and starting again. It was a variation on Ravel's 'Piano Concerto for the Left Hand'. I could hear the 'passion and intensity', as my father described it before sharing with me who Ravel composed it for: Ludwig Wittgenstein's brother, Paul, who lost his right arm in World War I. I was fourteen or so when my father shared this fact, and I recall the circumstances in which it happened. The piece in question had just been played on the radio one Sunday evening and the radio host had attributed it to another composer, and my father shook his head and said in a gentle voice, 'It's Ravel, you amateur,' and then he filled the rest of the evening with Ravel on his record player. It was strange hearing it in the middle of America, in that hostel on the road to see Gerard Hopkins.

I looked down as though a picture of the pianist below would form and explain that bloom of culture in the middle of nowhere, but instead the music stopped.

I heard a bang. Someone had slammed something. Perhaps the piano lid? Then the sound of a door opening down-stairs. And someone coughing outside. I looked out again and saw a lone man crossing the grounds towards the path that ran through the cornfield. My God, I exclaimed, it's Paul Wittgenstein! He was missing an arm. I saw the right sleeve of his white shirt flapping. His black suspenders held up his trousers so tightly it looked like they were lifting him off the ground. There, where the field began and the clearing stopped, he stood for a few minutes and turned around.

Of course it was not Paul Wittgenstein, who died in 1961. The man outside had both arms intact. He was wearing a shoulder sling that was supporting his right arm.

About an hour later, on the way out, I saw him smoking outside. He had changed into a light-blue collarless shirt with the same suspenders holding up green tweed trousers. There was a blue, heavy-looking duffel bag on the ground, in front of him.

When I passed, heading towards the red Prius, he spoke, pointing west, 'Hey, brother, going that way?'

'Pardon?' I pretended I'd not heard him. He approached, his steps heavy as though restrained by gravity. He wanted to know if he could ride with me.

'I'm headed to Council Bluffs,' he said.

'Oh,' I said, trying to see through this stranger with the sunburned face and chapped lips.

He tossed the cigarette butt and waited for my reply. I con-templated a lie that sadly refused to come. I found myself agreeing, 'Sure, why not.'

''Preciate it, man,' he said, and I caught a glimpse of his yellow teeth.

He lifted the bulging duffel with his free arm. He followed me to the car, tapped on the trunk and I opened it. He loaded his duffel.

'Those babies follow me everywhere,' he said when he climbed in to the car. He looked at me with a stare that suggested I say something, perhaps follow up on his 'babies' allusion, which I was yet to grasp.

'Oh, nice,' I said.

'Yeah, I've got three semis and two little ones back there.'

It took me a while to realise he was talking about guns.

He went on about them, detailing their technical dimensions as if I should already know. He was all casual and chummy. Just one guy discussing weapons with a total stranger.

'Oh, how nice,' I responded as casually as possible.

'Boston, eh?'

'Pardon?'

'Coming from Boston?'

'Ah, yes. Good ol' Boston,' I said, wanting to sound calm. 'And you, from around here?'

'Oh, no,' he answered and looked out the window.

He went on to introduce himself as Steve. He was going west, taking it slowly one state at a time until California, after which he planned to cross over to Mexico. 'Off to Meh-heeee-co,' he said with a tinge of wanderlust in his voice.

I detected something more, an undercurrent in the way his voice broke between sentences. I suddenly found myself wanting to know more, to ask a few questions, but I was deterred by the thought of his 'babies' lying in the trunk. Better to let things unfold naturally.

'Mek-zee-ko,' I said in a sing-song voice, trying to sound as relaxed as possible, and then I fiddled with the car radio.

A preacher's voice came up: … *and God said to Peter, son, arise, kill and eat.* I tuned to a different station: *Now we will hear a piece composed and performed by fifteen-year-old Brian Wilcox from Nantucket.* I left it, and Brian's composition for the piano filled the car, silky in its progression, with a hint of melancholy.

Minutes later, when one Darren Wilford, a cellist from Salt Lake City, began to play his idea of a Catalan lullaby, I fiddled again and landed on Rory Gallagher's 'I Fall Apart'.

'Now we're talking,' Steve said. 'Rory fucking Gallagher, just the fucking greatest.'

'Couldn't agree more,' I said carelessly, and let the radio play on.

Maybe it was 'Rory fucking Gallagher' or the sun that had grown warmer, but my hitchhiker was in a different mood, cheerful and excited, his voice rising as he spoke.

He saw Rory Gallagher in 1976. Not sure where. 'No, I remember now,' he said. He saw him at 'the Bottom Line in Greenwich Village'. He was nineteen or twenty then and had only been in New York for a month, straight from Carson, West Virginia, his hometown. Out to New York to do anything but work in the steel industry back home like his father and grandfather. He lasted only two months in New York before going back home. Tried Marshal University for a semester. Dropped out and took a job at a shipyard.

The radio DJ said something about Rory Gallagher's death, and introduced another track, 'Going to My Hometown'. My hitchhiker was still talking.

Seven years later he met a girl at a friend's party. They married shortly after and bought a house together. The first child came. Then the second and a third. He changed jobs. Became a foreman at a steel company. But 'it happened real fast,' he said, 'first they laid off a few workers, then they outsourced the whole thing.'

He went on and on about some grand corporate conspiracy. He said something about 'the one per cent' and a certain politician who 'takes it up the ass from corporate crooks'.

I sensed a different tone. He was speaking and pointing at the road ahead as if that politician and his corporate buddies were standing ahead, as if he wanted me to run them over.

'We should take those fuckers out one by one,' he said.

I was nodding my agreement, and suddenly my shoulders felt light and unable to control themselves. The steering turned left and we veered a little into the fast lane.

I regained control and steadied myself. Same old picture all around us: fields and big skies and a wide road. A green hauler passed, three small cars strapped to its back. A road branched off to the right. Steve carried on.

One thing led to another and he began to drink more than usual. He tried a few places but the jobs just weren't there. His children were growing up. His daughter already had a boyfriend, some shifty kid he didn't like, but what could he do? He thought things would normalise, that the jobs would return. He waited. Took odd jobs here and there. Time continued to pass. His wife, well, his wife…

There was a pause and I could almost sense a shiver running through him. He began to unbuckle his seatbelt, struggling. I tried to stay calm but I found myself speaking a bit too sharply. 'What are you doing?'

'Pull over,' he demanded, slapping the dashboard.

I pulled over.

He fumbled with the lock and got out.

Standing outside, just by the door, facing the cornfield, he surveyed the area.

I looked around as well, hoping to spot a shed or a house. Any sign of safety.

He unzipped his fly and began to urinate, after which he walked around to where his 'babies' were resting. He tapped the trunk. I looked in the rear mirror and could see a nasty expression on his face, his lips quivering. I had an impulse to hit the accelerator and disappear, leaving him there.

I saw him mouthing, 'Open the trunk.' I did. It took him a minute or so to pull a baby from his duffel, a pistol. He turned towards the cornfield and fired a shot. He fired another. And another. And then he released a long, animal scream.

You must flee the scene, I said to myself. Leave now, Frank.

I stayed.

It was over in a flash. He returned to the car, holding a half-empty bottle of vodka. He slammed the door shut. Sighed deeply and offered me a smile.

'Want some?'

'Nah,' I said casually. 'No drinking on the road. Ready?'

'Yes, hit the road.'

We took off.

'Sure you don't want a sip?'

'Why not,' I said, afraid I might upset him. 'Hell, the road is empty.' I said this in what I considered an American way of speaking.

'That's the spirit, brother. You only live once.'

He had already gulped a mouthful and offered me the bottle. I took a tiny sip. I tried the radio and fumbled through the stations for something buzzy.

I stumbled on Gnarls Barkley's 'Crazy'.

'Yes!' my hitchhiker exclaimed, hugging the bottle with his free arm. 'Some black shit, brother.'

'Oh yeah,' I agreed, 'some fucking black shit.'

He reached out and turned it up.

I pretended to enjoy it loud.

I entered the fast lane and accelerated.

In about five minutes I spotted a sign announcing a gas station ahead.

I accelerated even more, as if a prize awaited me there.

It was a small gas station, just off an exit, perching on an incline, a valley of grass behind. Two pumps. A small shop.

'I'll chip in for gas,' Steve said.

I declined.

I wanted him to stay in the car.

I wanted to breathe the open air alone. To stand alone.

'I'm not that broke, man. Let me fill the tank.'

I knew there was cash in his duffel. He had told me this. I also knew it was the vodka in him speaking. What if he sobered up along the way and demanded his money back?

He got out of the car and went to his duffel and came over with cash. Twenty dollars in two tens. I pocketed both notes and paid with the debit card that contained my stipends from William Blake.

We hit the road again.

'Want another sip?'

'Hell yeah.'

I gulped half a mouthful.

'Life is short, brother.'

I agreed with him, 'Life is indeed short.' I sang a made-up tune, 'Off to Mek-zee-ko, off to Mek-zee-ko.' He roared with laughter and reached out to tap my shoulder with his free arm. We became old buddies on the road. I suddenly had an impulse to ask why he finally left West Virginia. Life was tough, agreed, but how about his family, why leave them? I kept my curiosity to myself.

I was about to go for the radio when I heard an unmistakable sound. A police car with a lone flashing light mounted on the roof appeared from nowhere. It certainly hadn't been there a minute ago. He was probably hiding deep in the cornfields.

I pulled over. Steve hid the bottle under his seat and pretended to be asleep.

The officer was astonishingly tall, hunched. It was his 'baby' that set me on edge. Hoisted to his waist, his right fingers caressing it as though to warn me.

'Shit,' I whispered to myself, and suddenly every police-versus-black person encounter I had seen on TV or read about came tumbling through my mind. And there was the alcohol on my breath. Was I speeding? A fresh idea came to me: make sure he knows you're a foreigner, from Africa.

'Step out of the vee-hee-coo,' he said.

At his voice and accent, my heart sank. I pushed my strategy. 'Ai yam apening de dor arnd stehpin ouooot of dee carh.' I was shamelessly channelling Kabumba.

My hitchhiker released a pretend snore. I guessed he was suppressing a laugh.

'Goode arftarnoon sahh, orificer,' I said, stepping out of the car.

I sensed him softening. He had not expected the accent.

'Are you OK, son?'

My strategy was working.

'I yam okhey, sah, orificer. I yam from Uuugandah, visit my friend in Bosthorn,' I pointed to the hitchhiker, 'and weee goin toh his fahmeelee in Kansul Blaffs.'

'Ah, Uganda.' A generous smile crossed his face, and at once it seemed he no longer wished to be seen as an officer of the law but a warm friend, an American host. 'Uganda. That's over there in East Africa, right? You got that Lake Victoria there, right?'

'Raighte,' I jumped in, and declared that in fact I was born and raised in a little fishing village on the edge of Lake Victoria.

'Is that right? You know, my brother-in-law is a missionary down there in Africa, building churches. Best believers he ever saw. Built them a school in some village. Last summer he sent us pictures of the kids in their new uniforms. Melts your heart.'

'Yeesz,' I jumped in again, 'I laik meesshionaries. They breeng piss and hopiness.' I almost chuckled at the thought of 'piss' and 'hop'. My hitchhiker released another long, pretend snore. The 'orificer' did not seem to care about the man in my car. He was having a blast talking to me. Probably the first action of the day. And a great one for that matter – an exotic creature in the heart of America. The real deal. An authentic African. I wondered what would have happened if I sounded like Kevin Hart or Eddie Murphy. Maybe nothing more than a warning. But I sure didn't want to find out.

'Well, son, as you know, it's a free country here. But you gotta be careful. You were a little over the limit there. But it's fine. Go slower next time. How long you in America for?'

'Wahn mahnt,' I said, 'and ai goh bahck to Mbosituta.'

I still wonder how I came up with that name, Mbosituta.

'Mbosituta,' he repeated, solemnly, as if the good Lord himself was instructing him to say the word. 'Carry on, son. Enjoy this free country.'

He reached out and slapped my shoulder. I contemplated slapping him back or stepping forward to hug him. I restrained myself.

Back in the car, the joy of triumph gave way to dizziness. It felt like I had lost something, like I'd offered the officer everything I had, mind and soul and conscience. All I wanted to do was swallow a mouthful of vodka, pull back the seat, and sleep – like Steve, who was now sound asleep.

The police car reversed and disappeared.

I checked the distance to Council Bluffs. About thirty-five minutes to the exit.

I observed Steve. His face was as calm as a child's, almost pure, as though he had neither known nor seen any kind of suffering his whole life.

About ten minutes from our left turn towards the centre of Council Bluffs, Steve woke up and told me he was staying the night near some big casino and might spend the next few days trying his luck there, after which he planned to cross over to Boys Town, on the other side of Omaha. There was a twinkle in his eyes, an excitement inspired by expectation. A gambler. Could I drop him off at the casino? It was not far from the exit. The Hafta's. A hotel and all-in-one entertainment centre.

Well, why not? It would be a good chance to stretch my legs.

The Hafta's was a tall building. The tallest one in sight. I found a spot in a sprawling parking lot bustling with cars coming and going, Americans getting in and out: an athletic brunette in a glittering tight dress walking arm in arm with an enormous man in baggy shorts, a thick gold chain around his neck; a child trotting towards the main entrance with his parents walking behind; an elderly couple standing and gazing as if they had lost their way. The air was dry. I felt it on my skin.

Steve thanked me and, holding his duffel, looked longingly towards the entrance. All roads, it seemed, led to the glass doors of The Hafta's.

Standing next to him, I looked around the area and thought to myself, 'This, too, is the United States of America. These, too, are Americans, proud owners of a civilisation that frightens and mesmerises the rest of us from the distant and tired corners of the world.'

I smelled something in the air. The faraway smell of crude oil and manure, or something of that nature, like the smell of some parts of Port Jumbo after rain.

Before turning to leave, Steve came close and asked the real reason for my journey west. I thought of sharing the truth, that perhaps like him, I was trying to stay in motion until I found some sort of meaning somewhere, that I felt my destination – Cherry Springs in Nebraska – might hold something in store for me, that I was meeting Gerard Hopkins and so on. But instead I lied, afraid he might misunderstand me. It was a quick reflex, that impulse to lie; but I just didn't want to get a weird look from him, in case he could not imagine a Nigerian on a road trip in America. So in response to his question, I said a friend had invited me out to Colorado Springs for an international Christian conference. He nodded, wished me well, and left. I texted Perky: 'Somewhere in Nebraska.' And I stared at the phone for a while, hoping she would reply immediately.

I saw the tiny email folder blinking at the top of the screen.

I tapped to open the folder.

It was a Google alert about Kabumba.

I'd set up two alerts before leaving Boston: one for him and the other for Sara. The alert showed two links.

The first led to Kabumba's interview with a magazine run by the MFA students at Volumptia College: 'I'm NOT an African Writer, Says Ugandan Writer'.

The other led to an article on *The Bookdealer*'s website: 'African Writer Secures Book Deal in 10-Way Auction'.

Clicking on the first link, I was confronted by a picture of Kabumba in a three-piece suit. No Maasai toga. I read his interview. 'I'm a writer, good and simple, not an African writer. I write for the whole world. It's funny how *they* insist on calling *us* African writers because *we* are Africans, and *they* can exist as writers without this or that label. For the record, my forthcoming novel is NOT the African version of *Explorations of the Night*. Serge Verne's novel stands on its own – and my *Sisters of the Lake District* stands on its own.'

The article said Kabumba was recently awarded a new fellowship for emerging writers at the Latvian Academy of Letters. In Latvia, comfortably far from the sex workers in Uganda, the subject of his novel.

I checked his Twitter page. He had updated his profile: *Author of SISTERS OF THE LAKE DISTRICT (forthcoming) / William Blake Fellow / 1st Black Fellow @latvianacademyofletters. Rep @sinclairdavisliterary.* And he'd pinned a tweet about 'sitting on' the 'news' of his book deal 'for a while', how 'this is a big win for the #worldwide community of #POCs and #BAMEs'.

I scrolled through his retweets and saw that the programme was 'proud' of its 'fellow who had landed a deal', and I knew this was posted by Perky who handled the programme's social media presence.

I clicked on the link on Kabumba's pinned tweet and it landed me on *The Bookdealer*'s page, where I saw another picture of Kabumba in a light-blue collarless shirt, standing next to his literary agent, the notorious Sinclair Davis, who had already sold rights to Kabumba's novel to eight publishers around the world.

I studied the picture of both men. I was intrigued by Kabumba's transformation. I searched the smile on his face for clues. He looked as confident and comfortable as ever. He oozed the same charm, Maasai toga or not. And there was that hovering sense that he could pull everyone in his direction, selling them whatever he had in stock. I wondered what his ultimate goals were. He was clearly onto something, I just couldn't place what it was. But for some reason, as I sat there in that parking lot in Nebraska, I wished him well and returned to my journey.

16

SOMEWHERE after Omaha, a kind of memory rinse washed over me. It must have lasted a whole minute. A total erasure of all I'd seen and experienced along the way from Boston. All I saw in that moment was the road ahead of me. The fields on my right and left. The buzz of motion, of the vehicle dragging me forward. I felt my muscles relaxing. It was a wave of calm before my mind returned to its usual state, dredging up and amplifying my encounters and experiences along the way. A single memory stood out: a recollection of the short detour I took to see Barry, Indiana, a small town south of Lake Michigan and the birthplace of the modernist writer Harry Goddard. I still remember how scared I was by the ghostliness of the place, houses abandoned, lawns that had become little forests. I must have spent a maximum of fifteen minutes there in what I had thought would be a refreshing detour. Driving out, depressed by how neglected the whole town was, how it reeked of systematic abandonment, a remarkable sight caught my attention: a shirtless young black man playing the cello, accompanied by an elderly white woman on the violin. Their audience: a small group of people of all races, solemn, nothing fancy.

The stage: the wide porch of a run-down house. I reversed and parked across the street, wound down my window, and at once felt the visceral tug of the cello, as if the shirtless boy was drumming his fingers on my chest. I couldn't tell what the piece was, but it sounded like a cover of some popular hip-hop number. I got out of the car, crossed the road, and stood next to a man reeking of marijuana. He offered me a sombre nod. I could see tears streaming down the face of the cellist as he plucked and bowed away. His instrument spoke so many languages, so many silent words that landed on my heart with a gentle thud. And the violin caressed those silent words, fanned them out. It was both sensual and poignant. The cello began to cry a heart-wrenching solo, a procession into the dark. And when it was over, a small speech was made: a black boy was shot by the police, one too many, one too many, one too many, and it must stop, and it must stop, they must stop killing our brothers, they must stop killing our sons. I kept my eyes on the young cellist. A black boy with his cello, with his music, with his art. I could not tell what I was feeling at that point, but it all rolled into a type of anger I didn't understand, that I did not know where to direct, that I felt too ill-informed to sort. What would I say if asked to speak to the dead boy's mother? Sorry for your loss, ma'am? To what extent was her loss mine? I wanted to feel something more personal, something that said, 'It could've been you, Frank Jasper.' But I knew that my anger was diluted by a remote consolation that I would sooner or later leave the US to its woes; that I would go back to my own corner of the world with its familiar horrors. It was that consciousness of being a foreigner, a traveller, a stranger, that punctured what I was supposed to feel as 'a brother'. Frustrated and feeling like an imposter among true mourners, I returned to the red Prius and drove away.

17

F ROM Grand Island, the highway dipped and descended towards Kearney. I distracted myself by counting the exits on both sides, reading out their names – Alda, Wood River, Shelton, Gibbon – and wondering what these places looked like. Would I be the first Nigerian to move to Gibbon? What would my daily life look like in Wood River? How would I participate in community life in Shelton? How long before I began to feel at home in Alda? Would the people there, the 'natives' of Alda, help me settle in or regard me with suspicion? Would they let me come close, study them, smell them, touch them, observe them, write about them, place them in a web of patterns? Probably not, and for good reasons.

I had a professor who admired Lévi-Strauss, read Lévi-Strauss, wanted to *be* Lévi-Strauss. In his free time, when not teaching courses in English literature, he travelled to villages in the interior, interviewing people, sometimes staying for days listening and learning. He was working on a book of patterns. To make sense of the world in the interior. He disappeared one day, in the creeks, never to be seen again. It was the same professor who said migration was *the* great equaliser. When people migrate, he said, especially when forced off their land by difficult circumstances, they shed old hierarchies and begin a new life, collectively regarded by their hosts as newcomers. I recall thinking he had a point but wondered if he wasn't missing some other point; some refugees or migrants carry with them, on their bodies or in their minds, the currency to start with fewer obstacles than others.

Somewhere after Gibbon, I turned the radio on, listening to the news for the first time in many days. There were refugees drowning as they tried to cross to Europe from North Africa; there were refugees trapped at the US–Mexico border. The world had stayed the same. I was not missing anything. I tuned away from the news, landed on NPR, where a British-Gambian architect based in New York was talking about his new project in Florida, and going on about his very international background, growing up here and there, dragged from one European city to the other by his diplomat parents. He reminded me of Sara. They were of the same world, where you strategically announce your social status by downplaying the same. I switched the radio off. Edna and Allen crossed my mind.

The day after my 'trial', two days before leaving Boston, Allen texted to invite me to one of his 'spring rituals', an overnight 'cleansing' at Forest Hills Cemetery, where e.e. cummings and Anne Sexton were buried. I agreed. I was out and about in town. And when the time came, I took the train back to Forest Hills, following Allen's instructions which he'd sent over in three text messages: 'The cemetery is divided into streets and avenues. Go straight on Rural Ave, steer right on Cypress Ave, and left on Lake Lane, which runs along a small pond to Fountain Ave. When you hit Fountain Ave, go right for a few steps and look left. You'll find Chadwick's mausoleum. Can't miss it. I'll be hiding behind...' And *there* he was, between the mausoleum and the small hill into which it nestled, smoking a joint.

'I'm waiting for night to fall,' he said when I arrived.

I leaned against the mausoleum. It was green and lush all around, with trees and shrubs lining each lane, each avenue, each street, as though to shield the dead from the sun.

'So, they finally kicked you out, eh?' he said when I got there.

'Well, I saw it coming,' I said.

'It's probably a good thing,' he said, smirking, 'you never struck me as the residency type.'

He took out a book from his tote bag and began to read as if I wasn't there. I recognised the book. His scholarly edition of cummings' *Tulips and Chimneys*, published by the University Press of Western Mass, with an introduction by the eminent cummings scholar Richard Chester, who, as Edna once told me, had recently left his wife for Allen's ex-girlfriend.

Night fell.

The cemetery workers were gone.

The cemetery was empty. And like bats we emerged and walked back to Fountain Ave, which was just left of Lotus Path, where three phallic gravestones stood like palace guards.

We turned right, climbed a small incline on the grass.

He led the way. I followed, and soon we were there, at the site where the ritual would begin, a small circular slab on the ground, surrounded by dry leaves and pebbles left by visitors: EDWARD ESTLIN CUMMINGS, 1894–1962. Someone had left a box of matches and a pack of cigarettes, both beaten and faded. There were coins and pencils. We sat on either side of the grave, facing the road below, and the pond was visible to our left.

Sandwiches and grapes appeared from Allen's tote bag. He'd instructed me to bring the booze. There was a bottle of whisky in my satchel, and potato chips.

As was his custom, we ate in silence, which was fine by me, except that it gave room for the dean's voice to resume its torture, and with each bite I could see the dean's mouth moving, his shoulders rising and falling with every point as he read me the decision the committee had reached.

A cool breeze came and passed, setting off a chime in the distance. Allen ate like an animal, holding the food close to his mouth, hurrying it into his system, breathing heavily. I wondered if it was part of his ritual, filling the silence with the noise of mastication.

Done, we passed the whisky between us. He started rolling a fat joint and broke the silence. 'So, Frankie, tell me, what are you going to do now? Go back to Africa?'

He lit the joint. 'Or we could start a small press together,' he added.

It didn't occur to him that I would need a permit to stay and work in the US, that I had to account for every single minute I spent in his country.

'I'll drive out to Nebraska,' I eventually answered, 'spend a couple of days with my dad's old friend… maybe write something, I don't know.'

At midnight, Allen stood up and went closer to the pond. He took off his clothes. I did the same. The moon was up and bright. We stood facing the pond. Ripples formed and dispersed on the surface. The place was silent, yet I felt there were voices chanting inside me.

He stretched his hands forward. I did the same. He began to speak into the night, into the void, reciting words, long lines, each beginning with a word in Latin. His words were abstract, heavily referential, cadenced. I could barely make out any meaning, but I found myself transfixed. He was speaking to himself, to the space within, a private speech, and I could see how it transformed him, how he seemed lighter, freed from the anxieties that weighed him down, free from the world of the living, communing both literally and figuratively with the dead.

After he'd finished his ritual, he turned and began to walk on the path around the pond. I followed him. He broke into a quiet jog. We did the loop twice and retired where we started, camping out there until we both fell asleep.

We woke up around seven in the morning. Perky had left me several voicemails. I texted her to say I was back at my place and needed time alone, that I'd see her later in the day.

Allen and I picked up our trash. He rolled himself a last joint. Around eight we left the cemetery for his place in Roslindale.

He stopped at the liquor store on Hyde Park and Blakemore and bought a cheap bottle of vodka. At the Budget Mart on Blakemore and Florence, he bought hotdogs and said something about his money running out.

In Dale Square, we saw a small pop-up market in full swing. 'It's one of those farmer's markets where everyone and everything gives the impression of extreme happiness and social awareness,' Allen said.

We walked in but didn't last a minute, unable to survive conversations about rare tomatoes and lotions made from butterfly excrement.

We got to Allen's apartment.

He drank from the bottle of vodka. And soon was too soaked to talk.

He fell asleep.

I called Perky and said I was coming over. I left a note for Allen.

Before leaving, I scanned his room again – a single bed, books everywhere, a wardrobe, a door leading to a tiny kitchen, a framed picture of small Allen in a sharp suit standing between a dapper-looking man and a woman in a hat. An only child, like myself. A pathetic creature, like myself. I hurried out the door, knowing it was probably the last time I'd see him.

On Washington Street, towards Forest Hill Station, I stopped for breakfast at a small Dominican sandwich shop, just a block away from a run-down brick building that had caught my attention with the inscription above it: *Puritan Ice Cream Co., established in 1905.*

I ordered a Havana Cubana, ate it fast and left.

Close to the train station, on the Washington Street side, I saw an entrance to the Arnold Arboretum. I'd read about the Arboretum and had once planned to visit it. It was now or never, I thought, and went in.

A stone by the side said I was on Blackwell Footpath, and the path itself curved into a flurry of trees. As I walked further the clacking and pounding of the trains at the station began to fade. Soon I was at the Bussey Brook Meadow with birds singing and crickets chirping, ticking and buzzing.

'Many birds stay in Bussey Brook Meadow all year. The others leave for warmer climates in the Fall and return to nest here in the Spring.' So said a sign on the left side of the path, on a spot near a clearing dense with brown leaves.

'Migration is difficult and risky,' it continued, 'but the benefit of better weather further south, longer days and more food makes the trip worthwhile.'

I squinted to read the rest of the text, which was gradually fading from exposure.

'Some birds,' it continued, 'travel long distances, crossing oceans and continents, while others make a series of short flights, stopping to rest and feed along the way.'

There were interlocked vines everywhere, on both sides of the footpath, leading me further away from the Washington Street entrance. Multiflora roses, wild grapevines, nightshades, black swallow-worts, poison ivies, Japanese bittersweets, Virginia creepers.

I reached the end of the footpath, went through the gate, crossed South Street and re-entered the Arboretum through the South Street entrance. It began to rain. I stood under a heavy oak tree. And when the rain passed, feeling more and more exhausted, I decided against further exploration and went straight to Perky's place.

18

I N Barney, Nebraska, I stopped for coffee at a small café.
Alone inside, on my second Americano, I swept the area
with my eyes, unsure what I was looking for. Telephone poles
and wires running the length of the street like giants holding
hands. A Red Lobster on one side and an Old Chicago on the
other. Silence, overwhelming, disrupted now and then by the
fading sound of cars in the distance. For once, I was not dealing
with eyes staring at me, trying to understand or make sense
of my presence. No eyes digging to know who or what I was.

Taking the exit to Barney wasn't planned. I was, in a way,
driven off the road by an uncontrollable urge to write, an urge
that began when I spotted the Archway, a museum slash monument that rose above and across the highway like a footbridge.

Curious to know what it was, I had pulled over. The
museum was closed. I looked it up and the internet said it
was 'an enduring tribute to the adventurers who travelled
the Great Platte River Road though Nebraska and helped to
build America'. It was, in sum, the story of America: the push
to create something new.

Back in the car, I found myself thinking about the courage and grit of those early settlers out there in the middle of

America, the sheer panic of moving into the unknown. I also thought of the violence contained in that history, the violence of encounter, the violence of reinvention, the violence of constructing and fortifying a myth of origin.

Trapped in this mood, I felt compelled to write about my experience, to capture that joint feeling of admiration, fascination and repulsion.

I sent a quick email to Belema, my agent slash publisher, with the subject line 'Potential Memoir', and said I would like to write about my journey, how it was bringing me face to face with the true meaning of striking out to reinvent the self.

He replied a few minutes later, saying he'd known I would come round to writing something. He informed me of my place among writers who visited the US, behaved badly, but eventually got a book out of their experience. He reminded me of Joshua Ibitoye, the Nigerian poet and playwright who was awarded a fellowship to a university in Ohio in the sixties but was swiftly thrown out for not engaging, absenting himself from seminars and vocalising his views on American culture and politics in a period charged up by Cold War politics and the Civil Rights movement. He suggested a direct engagement with 'the American way of life', a memoir that compared it with life back home. And perhaps 'a chapter or two on race relations'. I tried to imagine a single word or set of words to describe that 'American way of life', a sentence that would compress it into a single narrative. My imagination failed me. And the expression 'race relations' sounded antiquated, like 'the Negro question'. Writing about race in America, I thought, would require a new insight, a fresh take to move 'the conversation' forward. The thought of inventing a new line of argument caused me much anxiety.

Cherry Springs, two hours north of Barney. I arrived early enough to catch the big sunset from Gerard's back porch. He was already out there when I pulled in and parked in the wide space to the right of his porch. When he hugged me, just before I sat on the wicker chair next to his, he said something I still remember when I think back to that moment: 'Welcome home, son.' He was a quiet man, almost cold, not in a way that caused unease, just that ability to maintain profound silence that comes from experience or the will to hold back, to advance slowly. Between both wicker chairs was a small table with a thick glass top, a copy of Gore Vidal's memoir, and a bottle of whisky and a single glass. The drink was for me. He stopped drinking a year ago, he said, after a minor stroke. At first he did not ask about my time in Boston, skipping that whole episode of my American experience as though it never happened, as if that part of the country did not exist. It was refreshing, the way he ignored it, which helped me to temporarily release myself from thinking about Sara and Kabumba, from agonising over my disgrace. He kept the conversation on the subject that connected us, my father, and the 'seventy-acre property' that he, Gerard, owned. His was the only house on the property, the next house was over twenty miles 'in that direction', ahead of us, where the sun was disappearing. And behind us lay nothing but a valley of grass and trees rolling for miles through acres of farmland. There was a garden and a chicken coop. 'I try to be self-sufficient,' he said.

The next morning, when I rose with the sun and went for a short walk down the valley, I saw his small patch of marijuana plants, which he had talked about the day before.

I plucked and nibbled a few leaves before walking on, and felt the morning breeze as it floated through me and through the trees and above the grass and into the valley ahead, visible in the leaves it touched, leaving acoustic registers that echoed inside me.

I stopped where a rock protruded from the ground.

I sat there and listened to the vast space in front of me, a valley that suddenly seemed animated by the rush of plains bison and by the passing of wagons and by the sound of death and agony. My head ached and I felt nauseous.

I stood up, and instead of returning to the house I pressed on and descended into the valley, walking further and further as the sun rose and crossed above.

I would repeat this ritual every morning for the number of days I spent in Cherry Spring, using the morning walks to digest what I was gathering about Gerard and the multiple lives he had led.

What I learned of my father was not shared directly. It was implied, done in a careful but deliberate manner: the brown envelope left on my bed containing a declassified CIA report on my father, compiled by one agent 'Death Valley' who 'tracked' the 'activities' of the 'young Nigerian maybe-communist from Nigeria', following him because he was an 'inroad' to the black bohemian world of London of that era, a link to the Afro-diaspora intellectuals from the British Colonies of the West Indies and Africa, and the African

Americans who moved between the UK and mainland Europe; and there was the notebook left on the reading table in my room, a photograph poking out from the page I believed he wanted me to see. The photograph showed a young Gerard standing next to the bust of what I assumed was a historical figure, and on the reverse side it read: 'Death Valley, Fitzwilliam Museum, Cambridge'.

I wasn't sure what I felt knowing that Gerard had been a spy and had used my father as an anchor. A part of me wanted to believe that at some point his work gave way to something more, something truer, as intimate as the narrative of their friendship showed.

I read the diary entry where the picture was inserted. It ran in multiple fragments, covering the days he and my father visited Harwich on the east coast of England, a year before they both graduated from Cambridge.

Both 'friends' had their separate reasons for going there. Gerard wanted to see where the 'two Christophers' lived: Christopher Newport and Christopher Jones. The former was the captain of the *Susan Constant* and a founder of Jamestown, the first English colony in North America. The latter was the captain of the *Mayflower*.

'In Harwich,' Gerard wrote, 'I asked around for Jones's house, and we were directed to the Alma Inn on King's Head Street and were told to look across from the inn. We did, and right there at 21 King's Head Street was a black plaque that said in white ink: *The Home of Christopher Jones, Master of the Mayflower*.'

The door was closed when they got there.

They knocked and no one answered.

'There was a little passage to the right', so they looked in through the gate and saw nothing but potted flowers in the backyard. Underwhelmed, they left, 'walking towards the River Stour, which flows into the North Sea at Harwich'.

They turned onto the quay, and just when they were about to ask someone for information about Newport, they saw a plaque, telling them that he 'was christened at St Nicholas' Church in Harwich on December 29th, 1561'.

And that was it, the two Christophers of Harwich and their small role in what became the United States.

For my father, as Gerard's diary showed, the reason for going to Harwich was to meet Randolph Stow. My father knew that the Australian writer was living there at the time. He'd read Stow's *The Merry-Go-Round in the Sea* and had corresponded with him.

Stow knew they were coming; my father had written in advance and received an invitation. 'He looked incredibly frail and quiet,' Gerard wrote in his diary, 'and evasive, picking his words carefully, as if an extra word might spill a dangerous secret.'

Stow was working on his novel *Visitants*. He told them about it in a single sentence, then he spoke about growing up in Australia, how he wrote his novel *To the Islands*. 'All these in short sentences separated by vast silences', during which they listened to the wind outside beating against the windowpanes and the sea heaving nearby.

Trying to impress the writer, my father announced that he'd memorised one of his poems, 'Landfall', and went ahead to recite it, a gesture that was 'rewarded with a dry grin and a nod'. I looked up the poem, and fell in love with it, especially the last two lines: 'And if they should ever tempt me to speak again, / I shall smile, and refrain.'

19

THE plan was to stay for two days and then drive to the airport in Omaha. I stayed a whole week and by the fifth night I had completed a draft of the first two chapters of *Cherry Springs & Death Valley,* a novel based on my father's relationship with Gerard, and Gerard's betrayal. 'This will relaunch your career,' Gerard said after he encouraged me to 'do a novel' out of the detail I now had. 'It will make up for Boston,' he said and winked. He knew about my 'career' and apparently knew about 'Boston' without my sharing anything with him.

I wrote from Gerard's point of view, the story of a black spy in Cold War Britain.

Under the name J.G. Bison, 'a retired secret agent living off-grid in the California desert', I pitched the first chapter of *Cherry Springs & Death Valley* to Sinclair Davis, noting that it was 'a novel of gay love and blackness and betrayal in the Cold War era', that it was 'based on real life', and to my surprise Davis's assistant replied and asked for an exclusive when the manuscript was complete.

I called my agent in Nigeria to break the news and he was furious that I had 'bypassed' him. Now that I was J.G. Bison, he insisted that 'we' do something with Frank Jasper.

In twenty-four hours he came up with a plan that stream-lined 'my unique American experience' into a 'programme of action for our mutual benefit'. After all, I wouldn't 'be the first to translate experience into money-making ventures'. There was a market and a need. I could make a good living filling that need. I was moved by his persistence, and I respected his honesty.

When I finally left Cherry Springs, I drove east to a town outside Omaha and checked into a cheap motel, where, for a week, I offered my Zoom workshops on anti-racism 'for those who could not be bothered'. My agent had listed me on several sites and the requests came flooding in, and when I saw how much we could make I was tempted to cancel my flight and overstay my visa for a month. I resisted.

On the connecting flight to Lagos, I caught myself thinking about something I read in my father's diary: that Gerard dealt with whatever issues he had by looking at himself in the mirror and addressing himself, the interviewer and the interviewee, talking himself through all the crises of history and civilisation, answering his own questions, the accuser and the accused.

'I once witnessed this experiment,' my father wrote, 'Gerard standing before his own image, speaking in two voices. "What are you?" asked a stern, hostile voice, to which a tender, fright-ened voice replied, "I'm not sure I know what or who I am. I exist in this body, and that is sufficient."'

I arrived in Port Jumbo at night and took a taxi straight from the airport to Jasper Street. When the taxi driver asked where

I was returning from, I told him and he nodded and wondered what I thought of America. 'Well,' I replied, 'it's a big country.' I knew there was only one answer that would satisfy him, that would slide into his existing idea of America. The America where every grain of sand was potential money. I didn't want to indulge him, so I said, 'It's similar to what we have here, there're all kinds of people.'

He laughed at my simple comparison, and said he had a cousin there who never wrote or called. He had a suspicion that his cousin had married a white woman, a move they'd warned him against, to stay away from 'those oyinbo women', because they were too much trouble. Not only did they turn you away from your family, but were also quick to shoot you if, you know, you tickled another woman.

A classic stereotype, I thought, and wanted to say something but found myself enjoying the driver's voice, the ring of pidgin English and its untranslatable nuances.

Dropping me off, he asked if I could pay in US dollars. I gave him a ten-dollar bill. He studied it, grinned, slammed it on his forehead for luck, held it out again and drove away.

Entering my room, I left my suitcase on the bed and went for the cigarette pack that was still lying where I left it. The note I glued to my desk years ago, after my first novel came out, was still there, a quote from Peter Ackroyd's *The Last Testament of Oscar Wilde*: 'There is something both magnificent and terrible about one's first book – it goes out into the world unwillingly because it takes so much of its creator with it also, and the creator always wishes to call it home.'

I lit a cigarette and went to the window.

243

It was pitch-black outside, with a few light bulbs on here and there, powered by small generators. 'Nothing has changed,' I whispered to myself.

The day after, still jet-lagged, I managed to go out for a walk.

I sniffed the air anew. The familiar buzz of the city was soothing, woofing through my body.

A line of beggars emerged from nowhere, holding each other by the shoulder, led by a man wearing dark shades, ostensibly blind.

It was a normal sight that I would ordinarily ignore. But in this instance, feeling generous, I handed their leader a dollar bill and he gasped, 'Dollah, American dollah.'

The currency had healed his 'blindness'.

I suppressed a laugh and strolled on, feeling good about myself.